A Harmony Falls Novel
Book 2

Battling the **Best Man**

ELLEY ARDEN

author of *Crashing the Congressman's Wedding*

CRIMSON
ROMANCE

F+W Media, Inc.

This edition published by
Crimson Romance
an imprint of F+W Media, Inc.
10151 Carver Road, Suite 200
Blue Ash, Ohio 45242
www.crimsonromance.com

ISBN 10: 1-4405-7233-X
ISBN 13: 978-1-4405-7233-3
eISBN 10: 1-4405-7234-8
eISBN 13: 978-1-4405-7234-0

To Susie, who has been the Alice to my Kory for ten fabulous years. Thank you for loving me, laughing with me, and supporting me. My life would be terribly dull without you.

Acknowledgments

Every so often in a writer's life, a person comes along and changes "the game." For me, that person is the incomparable Tara Gelsomino, who made me reach deeper than I ever thought possible and brought polish to my writing that I didn't know I needed. I am better because of her.

I also want to acknowledge my husband, whose medical career provided the details for Kory's career. He answered every random text, email, and verbal question with punctuality, professionalism, and a smile. He treats his patients with the same level of respect, and I am proud to be his wife.

CHAPTER ONE

What was it about weddings that made perfectly sane people act like lunatics?

Kory pressed her bare back to the padded chair, adjusted the wide black belt strangling her ribcage just below her breasts, and fluffed the ruby red crinoline skirt, trying to get comfortable at the bridal table. She wouldn't be caught dead in this dress for any occasion other than her best friend's wedding. And now that the beautiful wedding part was over, Kory was subjected to this...people she'd known her whole life bumping and grinding all over the dance floor.

The principal? Kory cringed as she watched Russell Stonewall hike up the polyester fabric of his pants so he could squat lower as some song from an era long before her birth urged him to shake his booty. She looked away, scanning the crowd for a reasonable distraction only to find her mother wiggling her breasts and strutting around Kory's rhythmically challenged father. This was so not reasonable. Kory pushed fingers to her lips to halt the dry heave that arose.

The bride and groom danced on the outskirts of the chaotic circle. Alice floated on a pure white puff of crinoline as she sang the song word for word to Justin, one hand wrapped around his ruby red tie. He was laughing at the performance, and Kory found her lips twitching, too. God, those two were made for each other, and seeing them happy was worth any amount of discomfort Kory had to endure being back in her hometown.

"Your mother can groove." The deep voice added too many ooh's to groove as it slithered down the table, invading Kory's personal space.

She crossed her arms and tossed Will Mitchell a humorless look. She'd been trying to avoid him all weekend, but was failing miserably. They'd shared a rehearsal followed by a dinner, and a two-hour photo shoot followed by a cramped limousine ride. It was damn near impossible for the maid of honor to avoid the best man.

What were the odds her best friend would marry the brother of her high school nemesis? Kory had happily avoided Will for the past twelve years, which had been surprisingly easy since high school graduation what with her stifling training schedule and hundreds of miles between them. She'd only come home for the occasional holiday, having parents who preferred she stay in Chicago and conquer the medical world. Alice and Justin's whirlwind courtship hadn't left much time for socializing when Kory had been home, but she was certainly getting her fill of Will now.

"What's wrong, Doc? Too much education to appreciate a little dancing?"

No. Kory just had no desire to look like a fool shimmying in a disco ball-lit fish bowl. She didn't get the allure of participating in something she wasn't very good at. It seemed like wasted time. Not that sitting here, trying not to be dragged into meaningful conversation with the smuggest asshole she'd ever met was any more productive.

"I don't see you up there," she said.

"True."

Silence filtered between them along with a sense of satisfaction that she'd shut him up so quickly. He'd never been easy to beat. Back in high school, Will had managed every science fair win; every standardized test high score; and the pièce de résistance, valedictorian. Try as she might, she could never top him. She'd been a merit scholar and the most academically decorated female graduate in the history of Harmony Falls High School.

"What more could you want, honey?" her mother used to ask.

Juvenile or not, Kory had just wanted to beat him. She didn't want her accomplishments quantified by her gender. She didn't want to be the best female anything. She wanted to be the best. Period.

She blinked, and those scenes from the past dissipated. Her medical degree trumped his MBA, didn't it?

Maisy Carmichael wrapped a boa around Gilbert Hoover's neck and pressed her fuchsia-clad body against him. Gross didn't begin to describe it. Kory sighed and reached a sweaty hand to her head, digging at a bobby pin Maisy had cranked into place several hours ago. Painful—this whole damn thing was painful. Minus Alice being happy, of course. And that was what Kory had to remember, not that she was uncomfortable in this dress and ridiculous hairstyle, not that people in this town had no shame when it came to dancing, and not that she was sharing a table with the man who, after all these years, still managed to drive her nuts. It was like some bizarre switch got tripped when she was in his proximity, one that managed to warp her love for healthy competition into something crazed. Heck, she'd about clobbered the guy with her bouquet when he'd managed to win that dumb bridal party scavenger hunt in the limo on the way here. It had been awfully suspicious that he just happened to have a penny in his pocket from the year the bride was born. Was he really that good or was he just that lucky?

He was a Mitchell, after all.

Kory glanced down the table, where he lounged seemingly in mid-execution of a formidable Ben Affleck impression—aloof but oddly attractive. It annoyed the crap out of her. His chair sat too far from the table, and he reclined in it, legs long and slanted, left arm slung along the back of the chair beside him. He was slouching, literally slouching, and that struck her as particularly annoying since he was a thirty-year-old dressed in a tuxedo. *Sit the hell up*, she wanted to say, but she bit her bottom lip instead and turned her gaze back to the dance floor.

Four beats of the music later, he was sliding into the chair beside her.

"How's Chicago?"

"Windy," she answered, her tone clipped. What she really wanted to say was, "Amazing, teeming with vibrant life and opportunity—things you don't have here." Because after all the time and effort the Mitchell family had put into saving this town from economic decay and population decline, the reminder they still had so far to go was bound to irk him. Irking him would feel good. But saying all that meant saying more to him than she wanted to, so she kept it short, but hardly sweet.

"You're doing some medical training thing, right? Alice mentioned it. How's that going?"

Medical training thing? Somehow Kory managed not to roll her eyes. "It's a traumatic brain injury fellowship, and it's challenging." In the best way possible. The move away from Harmony Falls to a major city had afforded Kory challenges and experiences she never would've found in this closed-minded little town, where the mailman had once informed her that men were doctors and women were nurses. As furious as that had made her, she considered the source. These people bought chewing tobacco in bulk and thought the first day of buck was worthy of a holiday. In one short month she'd be graduated from fellowship and ready to take her place as assistant medical director of the in-patient rehabilitation unit at the world-renowned Chicago Northern Rehab Institute. She'd have a prestigious title, a fat salary, and too many cultural experiences to count.

Beat that, Will Mitchell.

"So…uh…how much calculus do you use on a daily basis?"

She looked at him through squinted eyes, a pinch in her chest telling her exactly where this was going. "Excuse me?"

"You know, calculus? We were in that class together in high school." His grin turned wolfish as he gave her a very obvious once over. "Let me tell you. If you'd looked like this back then, I never would've passed."

Kory glared at him. Did he seriously not remember what had happened in that class? They'd *both* tested out of the usual Algebra classes offered to ninth-graders at Harmony Falls High—the only two in their class to do so. In Calculus, he'd been like a ten-year-old, poking his pencil between her shoulder blades, tugging on her ponytail, and cracking gum in her ear—but Kory hadn't minded. Will had been one of the cutest boys in the class and his playful teasing had made her feel special, like they were friends, facing a senior-level math class together. She'd found the attention from an attractive, smart, and charismatic guy charming.

Not charming, however, was the way it escalated. Unlike Kory who didn't even like to raise her hand in class, gregarious, funny Will had been able to fit in quickly and easily with the senior boys. After a few weeks, his new friends started teasing her too, but without the playfulness Will had. Instead, they cracked overtly sexual jokes that made her crazily uncomfortable. *Kory, what do math and my dick have in common? They're both hard for you.* That one had brought her to tears. Anger at their taunts and disappointment that Will—whom she'd thought was her friend—hadn't stood up for her but had laughed along with them made her even more withdrawn. The teacher and principal got involved and punished the boys, but it had been as if Kory was punished, too. Despite her ability to handle the classwork and her protests, the principal had also transferred her back to Honors Algebra. Will had remained in calculus, the only freshman in a senior-level class. And she hated him for it.

Once, when Will was without his entourage, he'd stopped her in the hallway between classes, and she'd suspected he was going to apologize, but she'd walked away before he could say a word—she'd felt too betrayed to accept an olive branch. He'd barely spoken to her after that, which was probably best. By then,

Kory didn't trust him, and she had vowed revenge, working extra hard to beat his scores.

Thankfully, things were different now. Dr. Kory Flemming was successful in a male-dominated field, which meant she hadn't so much as blushed in years. Whatever Will had hoped to accomplish by bringing up the calculus topic tonight wasn't going to happen.

With a shove, she pushed away from the table and stood. "Calculus," she said with a bitchy grin. "I remember it well. I learned a valuable lesson in that class."

"What's that?" he asked, smiling up at her.

"That you're a dick." She spun around on the bare balls of her feet and charged the dance floor.

• • •

Will watched her go, the smile fading from his face. First words she'd said to him all damn weekend and she'd insulted him. Then again, he probably deserved it. His booze-soaked brain had been scrambling, trying to come up with something, *anything* that might get more than a one-word answer from Kory. He'd succeeded, but at what cost? After that hostile exchange, he wasn't likely to get another word out of her for the rest of the night. What a shame.

They'd been friends when they were little. Teachers were always sticking them together for some project or another. But by high school, they'd gone their separate ways. The truth was Calculus was the only class he could think of that they'd had together. And apparently it was a sore point. That or Kory didn't take kindly to his attempt at flattery. Although she was definitely better looking now than she had been in high school, he probably should've tried a subtler compliment.

Shit. He thought about going after her, because Alice would read him the riot act if she thought he was being mean to her best friend, but he didn't trust his liquored-up self not to say something even worse, maybe something about tangent curves. After all these years, he didn't know her very well, but from the way she reacted to his previous come on, he wouldn't be surprised if a similar comment came with a slap across his face. Besides, watching her now, he couldn't see many curves. From the top of her bronze head to the tip of her honey-colored toes, she was long and lean, straight and strong.

She grabbed her mother's hand and then her father's and the trio did some awkward square dance move, shrinking the circle and then widening it again to the rhythm of a popular rap song. Will hoped she was a better doctor than she was a dancer, a thought that had him chuckling against the rim of his whiskey glass. He knew she didn't want to be out there, but the alternative was being here with him, and apparently that was a worse kind of torture—because he was a dick. Flinching, he swallowed another hefty mouthful of liquor.

The alcohol burned a path from his throat to his stomach, and he sucked cake-scented air into his nose. He caught sight of his smiling brother, and managed to smile, too. He was happy for Justin and Alice. He really was. But he would've been even happier had they eloped.

Justin approached from the opposite side of the table, and reached for his water glass. "You mean to tell me out of all these beautiful women you can't find one to dance with?"

Will looked at Kory, which was a laughable direction for his attentions to take. After their exchange, she'd be the last beautiful woman in this room to dance with him. Hell, she'd already managed to weasel her way out of their one official dance by partnering with the ring bearer and insisting Will dance with the flower girl.

He glanced at his brother. "If I'm dancing, I can only appreciate one of them at a time. From this vantage point, it's equal opportunity admiration."

"You're full of it." Justin skirted the table, and sat. "One of these days you're going to realize there's more to life than hefty profit margins at work and an Australian Shepard in your bed."

"Never." Will opened his mouth for an extra-large swig of whiskey.

Justin's hand landed hard on Will's shoulder. "I used to think success was measured by bankrolls and titles, too, but look at her."

The *her* Justin referred to was Alice no doubt, and Will obliged, scanning the dance floor until he found his smiling sister-in-law.

"She glows," Justin said. "She literally lights up my life. Before her, there was only darkness."

Will looked at the water glass in Justin's hand. "Please tell me you've had more than that to drink, because if you're saying all that sober, after Morgan Parrish cheated on you and made your last attempt at a wedding a laughing stock, while—may I remind you—simultaneously destroying your congressional career," Will said, shooting an incredulous glare at his brother, "I might just have to smack you."

Justin whistled. "First of all, that's ancient history, and second, damn, it's no wonder you're sitting alone. You're a real downer. You need to work on that, bro. This is a wedding."

"Yeah, a wedding. It's a fairytale for one night. But it isn't real." His gaze automatically skipped to his widowed mother who sat alone at a nearby table. "Reality is the so-called lucky ones finding somebody tolerable, getting married, and annoying the shit out of each other for decades, until one of them finally dies, leaving the other one an emotional void."

Dad had been dead for decades, but Will remembered what their mother had been like before cancer obliterated the man. He had a singular, sharp memory of her sitting at their long dining table with Aunt Dorothy, laughing until she cried, her whole body shaking at some joke. He'd never heard her laugh like that again. It was like she'd shut off everything the day Dad died—the laughter, the warmth, the love. All she lived for now was the family business. Will tucked a finger into his shirt collar and pulled, making some room for the next swallow of whiskey.

Justin stared at him for a long moment, and then shook his head. He drained his water glass and stood. "Before I return to my glowing bride, who is infinitely better company than you, let me remind you that even when our father was alive, our mother was never a naturally happy woman, and despite all the bad things that happened to me, I'm here, happier than I ever dreamed I could be." He squeezed Will's shoulders. "I'd rather be mayor of Harmony Falls with Alice by my side than President of the United States with Morgan Parrish any day. Sometimes when you lose you win." After one more squeeze, he walked away.

Will sat there, polishing off the whiskey. His gaze wandered back to Kory who seemed to be using her parents as a shield, but not shield enough for him to lose sight of her completely. Her long arms remained locked at the elbows, and her bare shoulders were tight and square. He pushed fingers against his throat and rubbed at some sort of discomfort as she tossed her head side to side, the blunt ends of her straight hair whipping her jawline.

She looked at him, an icy glare that changed before she looked away. It didn't soften, but it definitely lost some of its intensity. And when she looked at him again—fast enough for him to miss it if he blinked—it was something else entirely. Pricks of pleasure scattered across the back of his neck and crawled onto his face. And they were perplexing as hell, because she hated him. Didn't she? She'd barely talked to him all weekend.

Let's think about this for a minute... But the liquor melted more than everything in its path, turning his belly into a bucket of jelly and his brain into a dehydrated sponge. He reached for an unattended plate of wedding cake and polished it off.

"I totally take offense to people not dancing at my wedding." Alice seemed to come out of nowhere, plopping down in Kory's chair and grabbing the long-stem glass of champagne Kory had neglected.

"Did my brother tell you to come over here and *glow* on me so I'd quit being a wallflower and find a suitable dance partner?"

"He may have mentioned you being moody." She drank, leaving a vivid lipstick print on the rim. "I also saw you talking to Kory, which didn't seem to end well. Were you picking on her again?"

"More like reminiscing," Will lied, dropping the fork and rubbing a palm against the back of his overheated neck. He told himself not to, but he lifted his gaze to the lady in question. She was still dancing, if that was what one could call it. It was more like jerking with a little thrusting thrown in, and...*damn*. He closed his eyes and shook his head.

"You know, if you keep picking on her, she's going to think you like her."

His nose twitched as he looked at his new sister-in-law. "We're not in elementary school, Alice."

"Exactly. So grow up, Will. Stop looking like you want to pass her a note that involves checking yes or no." She swatted his arm and threw back her head for a cackle. "Or is that how you ask all your dates out? Because it might explain why you never seem to have any..." She batted pitch-black eyelashes and pursed her lips.

He did not want to talk about his lack of a meaningful social life or the fact that he felt more comfortable with things he could measure and compute. Who wanted to spend life tethered to something abstract like what another person thought and felt? It was too subjective for him—too ripe for real rejection. Fortunately, as a wealthy, decent-looking, single man, he didn't have to risk much to find a willing woman for his bed. The hard part was dealing with her disappointment when she realized he wasn't going to change his mind about having anything close to a relationship. That sort of thing just wasn't for him.

"I'm perfectly happy being single, Alice. I can work as many hours as I like, close as many deals as I can, and I don't have to worry about sharing the profits with anybody."

"Sounds lonely," Alice said, adding a pout.

If Will were being honest, he'd admit sometimes it was, but lonely was a hell of a lot easier than finding someone whose eyes didn't glaze over when he started talking about the law of diminishing marginal returns. That sort of reaction was no ego boost, and it was exhausting trying to hide part of him simply so he could keep somebody by his side. It was better to keep things casual. That way nobody got to know what was buried beneath the Mitchell polish.

"Come on." Alice stood and grabbed his hands. "Let's dance." She tugged, jumping to the disco beat.

Will stayed put. "Don't you have some theatre donor to schmooze?"

"At my wedding reception? That would be tacky. Besides, Justin is busy gathering support for his mayoral run."

Because *that* wasn't tacky. Will managed to keep his eyes from rolling while Alice ducked beneath one of his raised arms and twirled. She danced around him like he was reciprocating, and he suddenly felt like the miserable fool Justin had accused him of being. This was a wedding. His big brother was right; Will needed to work on his mood. He stood, smiling at Alice's shocked squeal when he spun her around again.

"There you go!" She pulled him away from the table. "Three more steps and you'll be on the dance floor."

He'd had just enough whiskey to make following her seem reasonable.

"I'm in shock." Justin said when they'd reached the dance floor.

Alice released one of Will's hands and laced her fingers with her husband's. "He's not as boring as you think he is."

Maybe not boring, but he sure felt like a third wheel. Will released Alice's other hand but not before he gave it a squeeze. "Thank you."

"You're welcome." She kissed him on the cheek. "But you're not allowed to sit down again. Got it?"

Will nodded. "I'm just going to find my own partner."

"Excellent. Our job here is done," Justin said, spinning his bride toward the center of the floor. "We'll be watching you."

Will shook his head and smiled at the goofy, wide-eyed look his brother gave, and then he set his sights on the crowd. There had to be someone who would tolerate his mediocre dance moves and not mistake his offer to dance for something more.

His mother still sat alone, surprisingly without his younger brother Mark, who was better known as her shadow. Asking her was probably the least complicated option.

"Mother," Will said, inclining his head when he reached her side. "May I have this dance?"

She wrinkled her narrow nose as she watched the dance floor. "I've danced enough for one night."

Will winced at the easy brush-off. He'd seen her dance exactly twice: once with Mark during the bridal party dance, and once with Justin during the mother-son dance. He didn't want to take it personally, so he told himself even two years after her heart attack, she hadn't regained all of her strength, but it was hard not to feel rejected. With hands in his pockets, he glanced at the full dance floor, having lost his drive to change his mood. Maybe he'd just sit here and talk business. At least his position and achievements as Chief Operating Officer of Mitchell Company, Inc. could be counted on to endear him to his CEO mother.

"I sent Mark for drinks," she continued, and then she looked at him. "Well, don't just stand there blocking my view. Either sit or move along."

On second thought, there had to be a better option for company.

"Enjoy your drinks," he said, deciding he'd rather deal with Justin and Alice's disappointment over seeing him back in his seat at an empty table than weather his mother's sour attitude and disapproval.

He'd only made it halfway across the dance floor, when Carole Flemming caught his eye.

"Will," she preened, sweeping toward him, dragging Kory behind her. "This is beautiful! Your family sure knows how to put on a wedding."

Money could do that for a person, money and Alice Cramer Mitchell's flair for the dramatic. He took a quick glance at the glistening red and gold ballroom and smiled. "Thank you. You look like you're having a good time."

"Oh, I am."

Kory was dead silent. She'd moved on from holding hands with her mother to locking elbows with the woman. And she was looking everywhere but at him.

"But I'm beat," Mrs. Flemming added. "Kory is suddenly an Energizer bunny."

On that comment, Kory's emerald eyes widened to full moon proportion. "Well, I…"

"Should dance with Will," Mrs. Flemming said, shoving her daughter toward him. "He doesn't have a partner. Do you, Will?"

Will shook his head. "I do not, and my brother and his new wife made it perfectly clear I need to find one."

Kory stepped back. "On second thought, I *am* tired."

"Nonsense." Mrs. Flemming smacked her daughter's hand a few times and pulled away from her grip. "Dance for heaven's sake. Once you get back to Chicago it will be all work and no play."

If Kory's teeth were nails, Will had no doubt she would've spit a mouthful at him.

"Come on, Kory. It's one dance. Don't tell me you're afraid I'll be so good I'll make you look bad."

"Hardly." She huffed but took a step closer. "One dance, Will, and only because I don't want to disappoint my mother, but I'm warning you. If you mention calculus, I'll knee you in the balls and walk away."

He chuckled. "Deal." Sliding a hand around her waist and pulling her closer, his laughter evaporated. For a skinny woman, she sure was soft, which may have had something to do with the miles of satin covering her. He opened his mouth for a shallow breath, drawing her the last couple inches against his chest, getting a mouthful of air tinged with something even sweeter than wedding cake. His rusty libido groaned. Somewhere in the distance beyond the physical sensations of Kory's palm pressing against the back of his neck…and her fingernails grazing his hairline…and her opposite hand nestled hot and tight in his…his brain whispered to his body, *she's not interested in you.*

Acoustic guitar music registered, and then her breath tickled his earlobe. He froze for a moment before instinct had him twisting his wrist and rotating her arm so he could hold her hand against his chest. Swallowing was inexplicably difficult, so he cleared his throat to aid the process, and felt her body tense.

He should've stayed at the table with his mother. At least he knew where he stood over there. Here, he was just a man, feeling things for a woman, who, he was damn near certain, wasn't feeling anything at all for him.

"You know, you can speak? When I said don't mention calculus, I wasn't suggesting we dance in awkward silence."

He nodded, loosened his fingers around her hand, and lightened his palm on her back. "I'm sorry. I'm trying to behave.

It seems like I say something stupid every time I open my mouth around you."

Tipping her head back, Kory studied him. Her brows pulled together, wrinkling her forehead, and her glossy lips pursed. She looked…beautiful. Will squeezed his eyes shut for a split second, trying to reset his brain.

"That's the smartest thing you've said all weekend." She released a bona fide chuckle that lit her green eyes and showed off the prettiest smile.

Will laughed, too, and that bit of cordial commiseration fanned the spark in his gut. *Bad idea*, his brain said. *She still doesn't like you.* But his body had a mind of its own, pulling her closer until she settled her chin on his shoulder and somewhat relaxed.

Apparently, sixteen years hadn't changed a thing. When Kory Flemming was near, Will Mitchell acted like a fool.

He noted the song winding down and battled a burst of disappointment, because he wasn't ready for her to leave—not when they were finally playing nicely. A few strands of silky hair brushed his lips, and he darted out his tongue, taking a not-so-innocent taste. He really was a strange bird.

"You know, when I get back to Chicago tomorrow night, I'm going straight to ophthalmology and requesting they zap my eyes with laser. Maybe they can erase some of the whacked out things I've seen since I've been back here." This was more than she'd said to him the entire weekend, and all he could take away from it was she was leaving tomorrow. He had no idea when she'd be back again, especially with her poor opinion of small-town Harmony Falls. And that felt like a terrible shame.

Suddenly, he wanted to alter their entire history or at least press rewind on the weekend. Maybe with more time he could've found his footing with her, and they could've had a little fun. After all, she was the only person he knew who might share his excitement over the discovery of a Higgs boson subatomic spec. Then again, if her mother was right, fun—scientific or otherwise—didn't seem to be a high priority to Dr. Flemming.

"Is it true what your mother said?" Will asked.

"What did my mother say?"

"That Chicago is all work and no play?"

"I like to work."

He could appreciate that. Heck, he lived that way, too. "You don't like to play?"

A charged silence lingered between them, and the music changed to a fast song not conducive to holding her close, but she surprised him by not backing away.

"I play," she whispered.

A hot flush greater than anything the whiskey had delivered heated Will from the inside out.

"Get a room," Mark called as he cut across the crowded dance floor, two highball drinks in hand.

That did the trick. Kory rocketed from Will's arms like he'd burst into flames—he felt like he did. She blinked fast and furious, adjusting the belt around her waist. "Thanks for the dance," she managed before scurrying away.

Will turned to his younger brother and glared. "Nice."

Mark laughed. "Here." He held out a small glass of amber liquor. "Consolation."

Will threw it back, because, hell, he'd rather be drunk and numb than wondering why he was hot for Kory Flemming after all these years.

CHAPTER TWO

After Alice tossed the bouquet and the happy couple departed through a storm of bubbles, Kory hid in the coat checkroom, helping Gertrude Cash connect guests with their predominantly outdated overcoats and shawls. She sat on a brown vinyl chair in the corner and counted safety pins and numbered tags while Gertrude talked about her latest litter of coonhounds. Mind numbing. But still better than whatever happened out on the dance floor. *That* was anything but numbing. *That* was…confusing and disturbing.

Was Kory really feeling something more than annoyance and disdain for Will Mitchell?

Gah! She tipped her hand and spilled a palm-full of pins into a jar.

"And this one has the cutest patch of black right above his little boy parts. Ooh! I have a picture." Gertrude jabbed at her phone's touchscreen.

Great. So because Kory couldn't be woman enough to face Will after their unsettling dance, she was going to subject herself to arguably more unsettling photos of a dog's genitalia. She was too old for this, too strong. That red-faced neophyte who strolled into a senior calculus class with the upper corners of her Trapper Keeper digging into the flesh beneath her breasts? That loser was gone.

Kory set the jar on the lower shelf beside her and swiped sweaty palms together. How long had she been hiding in here? She glanced at the gaudy clock on the wall above the counter just as Gertrude shoved the phone under her nose.

"Look at that. Isn't that precious?"

Kory almost looked out of a morbid curiosity she cultivated in medical school, but in the end, she didn't have to…

"Ladies, I'll be leaving now." Tubby Stanwick winked, and then slipped an unlit cigar between his raisin-like lips. "And don't forget my hat."

While Gertrude fawned over the ancient man—even showing him the outrageous photo of her puppy's "little boy parts"—Kory contemplated leaving the coatroom and at least retrieving her shoes. She started to glance at the clock again only to be interrupted.

"I'm going to walk Tubby out," Gertrude said, grinning. "You can manage for a few minutes, can't you?"

She had no idea how many people were still milling around the ballroom. Wasn't there usually a mass exodus after the bride and groom left? A few coats remained, stuffed at the end of the rack—a purple puffer, a fur stole, and a military trench coat. Kory doubted anyone wore any of those to this reception. It was June after all. They were probably unclaimed items. Considering that and the fact this reception was taking place in Harmony Falls where nothing criminal ever happened, she was probably in the clear to leave along with Gertrude. But she wasn't certain she wanted to leave the "safe room."

So she stayed a little longer, flipping through yellowed ledger pads, containing the history of garments in the room. Entries went back to 1989. Crazy. And the fact that someone logged a raccoon cap in February 1994? That was even crazier. This town…

"Excuse me. I have a jacket to claim."

Kory blinked, but didn't look up, because damn it, she knew that voice. It was the voice she'd been trying—and failing—to avoid.

"Let me guess. It's a purple puffer vest," she said, returning the ledger to the shelf below the counter, careful not to take her eyes off the weathered binding of the book.

"Nope. The fur."

She glanced at him, standing in the open doorway, a green ticket pinched between two fingers. "Fur seems a little ostentatious—even for you."

The balls of his cheeks rounded, but his face stopped short of a smile. "The fur is my mother's."

Seeing him again caused an onslaught of fresh nerves to interrupt the steady beat of her heart. "Sure it is," Kory said, turning her back to him and reaching for the stole. "You always were flashy, Will Mitchell." It wasn't meant to be a compliment.

"Are you really leaving tomorrow?"

The random question stopped her mid-grab. "I am."

"That's a shame."

Her skin prickled. "Why?" she asked, turning slowly, holding the stole between them.

He stepped into the room, exchanging the ticket for the fur. "It would've been nice to go out, catch up, you know, hang with an old friend."

The same blast of incredulity that led her to call him a dick and walk away earlier prompted a sarcastic laugh. "Are you serious? We aren't *friends*, Will! We haven't been *friends* since calculus when your *real* friends harassed me to the point I got pulled from the class." Each word had carried her a step closer to him until she was raging in his face.

He balked. "Come on, Kory." But then recognition flashed across his annoyingly handsome features. "You got pulled from that class?"

"Yes, I got pulled from that class. What did you think happened to me? I disappeared."

He snapped his fingers and nodded. "Yeah! Come to think of it I tried to ask you once what happened, but you walked away from me. You do that a lot, you know?" he added with a weak smile. "But apparently, you have reason to." He shook his head. "I honestly had no idea."

He didn't remember what happened. Figured. All these years—all the energy—she'd essentially wasted. It wasn't at all satisfying to swear revenge on someone who didn't know how badly he'd hurt her.

"Forget it," she said, dropping to the flats of her bare feet, suddenly surprised by their close proximity.

"No. This time, I won't forget it. I'm very, very sorry for whatever part I played in you being pulled from that class."

The seemingly heartfelt apology stunned her, stopping her before she could step back and put reasonable space between them. She stood there stuck in some strange mix of abhorrence and attraction. "It's okay, Will," she finally said. But the words weren't accurate. If anything were really *okay* her heart wouldn't be racing.

"It's not okay. Whoever I was in that class, I can assure you it's not the real me. If we had more time together, I could prove it."

His head tilted to one side. His tuxedo shirt opened at the throat. And he studied her with dark sparkling eyes, causing a hot spot low in her belly.

This attraction didn't make any sense, and Kory thrived on rationality. She hadn't trusted Will Mitchell for years. What purpose did it serve to let her guard down now? She'd be back in Chicago before her brain had time to process their interaction.

Then again, maybe that was the best part about it. Maybe that was why she allowed herself to maintain eye contact with him past the point of innocent interaction.

Will leaned closer, his voice just above a whisper. "So, would it ruin all our progress if I kissed you?"

"Only if it's a really bad kiss," Kory said, lifting her chin to within a fraction of an inch of his, smelling the whiskey on his breath.

Will's hands landed on her hips the minute his lips landed on her mouth.

•••

Only if it's a really bad kiss? After that lead-in, the pressure was on.

Will started soft, hoping Kory wouldn't change her mind, tugging gently on her bottom lip. She surprised him with tongue, and the kiss turned hot, wet, and hard. *Holy hell.*

"Heavens to Betsy, I almost forgot my coat!"

Will's brain didn't fully register the interruption until Gertrude Cash was standing right next to them. Kory bolted from his arms like she'd been caught stealing from the coat-check tip jar.

"Don't mind me," Gertrude said, moving to the corner of the room and freeing the purple puffer vest from its hanger. Will tracked her with his eyes, but his body remained zeroed in on Kory, bathed in heat she was still radiating. They'd barely had time for a proper kiss before Gertrude barged in. Even so, his brain hummed from the contact and he wanted so much more.

"Have a nice time, kiddos." Gertrude tossed them a yellow-teethed grin.

"Good night," Will managed.

"Wait," Kory rushed past him, eyes wide and watery. "Did you see a pair of shoes out there? I need to find my shoes before the clean-up crew grabs them." She bolted from the room, leaving him staring at Gertrude.

The woman zipped her vest and eyed him with raised brows. "I 'pologize if I screwed things up."

He exhaled out his mouth and shook his head. "Nah, you're good." Because what else could he say?

"Okay. See you tomorrow."

His thoughts collided with her words. "Tomorrow?"

"Isn't it tomorrow? I thought the nurses and aides at the home were meeting with you."

He nodded slowly as real life and obligations trickled into a consciousness marred by liquor and lust. Gertie had been an aide at Harmony Elder Care longer than Will had been making sure the wide array of Mitchell family businesses ran smoothly, and she was among the most vocal proponents for the nursing home's sale. In fact, only his mother seemed to want the transaction completed more. "Tomorrow. Yep. See you then."

She wrinkled her wide nose. "You got someone driving you home?"

He grinned. "Yes, I have a designated driver. Don't you worry."

"Good man." She slapped him on the upper arm and walked away. "And I'm sorry about barging in."

Will's lips twitched, and he swiped a finger across them. He was sorry, too. If the kiss had come to a natural, satisfying end, where would he and Kory be now? Would he still be headed home in a town car alongside Mark and Mother? Unfortunately, the answer was yes. If Will wanted to keep favor with his mother and anyone with a vested interested in the company's bottom line, he didn't have the luxury of pursuing his passion, especially one that was most likely a fantasy. Will had to be at work bright and early tomorrow morning. Reality included more than twenty local businesses under his family's direction, which meant while most of Harmony Falls would be sleeping off their reception stupors, Will would be holding a typical Saturday meeting, this one at the nursing home, which had fast become his least favorite asset in the Mitchell family portfolio. Between his mother's insistence that a lucrative sale come swiftly, and the twenty women who were counting on him to strike one hell of a compensation package deal with a stingy Valley Hospital System, his stress level was through the roof.

"Can I get my coat?"

Will turned to see Gilbert Hoover standing in the open doorway, and then he turned back to see the only remaining coat on the rack, some sort of military jacket. "Sure, help yourself. I was just heading out."

He patted the man on the shoulder as he pushed past him. Three steps into the ballroom, his brother and mother approached.

"Where have you been?"

Will glanced down at his mother whose curtly delivered question had him searching for a safe answer. He settled on, "Helping with coat check."

Mark chuckled. And before Will could drive an elbow into his brother's side, she settled between them, taking them both by the arm.

Flanked by two of her boys and with her chin lifted higher than humanly possible, she let Will and Mark guide her to the door.

While Will walked at a sloth's pace, barely lifting the soles of his dress shoes off the waxed wood floors, he scanned the empty room, looking for Kory, but there was no sign of her. He ground his back teeth together, frustrated he'd let his uncertainty around her waste an entire weekend.

"Are you sick?"

Will glanced at his mother, who was looking up at him. "No." He caught sight of Mark, grinning like a psycho clown.

"Then stop looking like you're sick." She pinched Will's bicep. "Stand up straight."

Mark's laughter was followed by a sharp, *"Ouch!"*

By the time they reached the town car, the small amount of excitement and intrigue that managed to seep into the weekend was a distant memory. The Mitchells were back to business as usual. Mother and Mark occupied the spacious backseat. Will sat up front with the driver.

"Thank God we're done with all this wedding nonsense." The Mitchell family matriarch wasn't one to mince words. "Now, we can get on with what's important. William, Rand Nelson says his mother's care is abhorrent in the home. The aides are mean to her."

Will gripped the door handle and stared straight ahead. "We've investigated her claims, and I can assure you, they are inaccurate."

"We can investigate all we want, but if a resident and her family feel they're being mistreated, then we have a problem. This is all the more reason to unload that asset, which is a liability in my opinion."

"Yes, Mother," Will said, ignoring the impulse to mention Mrs. Nelson and a dozen other residents would be homeless when he did. Mother wasn't one to sympathize.

"I told Bruce Carter you would meet with him about the vacant drugstore space."

Will shook his head. "I'm already in talks to lease the space to George Chompsky."

"Oh please! George can barely make the monthly rent in that closet of an office he has downtown. He'll never be able to afford that space at twice the square footage. No, Bruce's logging business is flourishing and he'll easily have the capital."

"Fine, I'll talk to Bruce," Will said, swallowing the emotion that came with knowing this wasn't going to end in George's favor. His mother was right, and usually Will wouldn't favor feelings over the bottom line, but in taking care of Will's dog, Molly, George had become a friend. He'd been the town vet for thirty years, and it wasn't his fault too many people in Harmony Falls were forced to pay for services in labor trade or baked goods. All Will wanted was to make the numbers work in George's favor as payback for the good he'd done, but Will should have known he wouldn't be able to pull it off. Those types of gestures were better left to Justin, the Mitchell son who was allowed to have a heart.

Twenty minutes later, Will walked through the door of his condo, already blissfully stripping off his jacket and tie. Some of the tension he'd acquired in the car disappeared. All things considered, he was a lucky man, maybe not as lucky as Justin, who was headed to the beach on an extended honeymoon, but certainly luckier than Mark, who was headed home with their mother. Somehow that poor bastard drew the short end of the stick.

Scooping an arm beneath Molly's belly, Will helped the ten-year-old Australian Shepherd onto the bed and stripped out of his clothes, leaving behind his boxers. The sheets were cold against his skin, and he tried not to think too much as he dropped his head to the pillow. He'd done enough thinking for one day. A few incomplete thoughts about tomorrow's meeting and the hospital takeover flashed in his mind. Molly snuggled against his left side, and he closed his eyes. Sleep. Will welcomed it with a heavy sigh.

Too bad he tossed and turned much of the night, dreaming about Kory.

CHAPTER THREE

If anything could make Kory wish away her return to Chicago, it was the smell of her mother's Applewood bacon. It wafted down the hall from the kitchen and she took a deep breath as she sprawled on her back underneath the quilt that had been a graduation present from Grandma Carter. Kory stared up at the faded NSYNC poster nailed to the ceiling. Justin Timberlake looked like he had boobs. She squinted, reached for her glasses on the bedside table and pushed them up her nose. Okay, so they weren't boobs, just oddly defined pecs. She blinked the haze from her eyes as she glanced at the rest of the crew. They were all so awkward. And yet, they were hanging on her ceiling. In her defense, she'd been fifteen years old when she drove in those four nails under Alice's watchful eye, and fifteen-year-olds weren't very smart—they made decisions with overactive hormones.

Kory's slow-to-start brain conjured an image of Will. Certainly, he had better pecs than Justin Timberlake. *Crap.* She did not want to be mind-ogling Will Mitchell's pecs. Even if they were the greatest pecs known to man, there wasn't a thing she would do about it. The wedding was over, and so should be the erratic thoughts and behavior that led her to kiss him.

Apparently, thirty-year olds weren't much smarter than fifteen-year-olds.

Lifting a leg over Smith's snoring body, Kory shimmied from between the dogs. After smoothing Wesson's fur, she pushed off the mattress, a little surprised they were still with her, considering bacon smelled up the house. Their devotion despite her eighteen-month-long absence was sweet.

The minute she stood, they hopped off the bed and stretched while she threaded arms into her robe and guzzled from the glass of water her mother never failed to set on the desk. She unplugged her phone from the charger, scrolled through emails, deleted a few, saved the rest for later and flicked over to Facebook, where Alice was posting pictures from the drive to the beach. Most were too blurry to appreciate, but Kory smiled anyway, happy Alice's dreams had come true. It was a sappy notion, made sappier by Alice's proclamation she was living her fairytale. Kory didn't believe in fairytales, at least not ones that ended with white knights in luxury cars who opened their checkbooks and magically solved life's problems. Of course, she'd never tell Alice that, especially not now that the white knight turned into a husband.

To each her own, Kory thought as she dropped the phone into her front pocket and cinched the belt around her waist. She was married to ambition, and she liked it that way.

The dogs trotted from the room, no doubt aware of the bacon now that they were up and moving around. Kory drew a deep breath and held onto the heavenly scent until her mouth watered. She was going to enjoy this meal—her last home-cooked food before she headed to the airport and back to Chicago where she lived on protein bars and coffee in paper cups. Wesson bounded down the stairs ahead of her, but Smith didn't follow. He stopped half in and half out of Mom and Dad's bedroom, his tail tucked between his legs.

Kory patted her thigh. "Come on, boy. Bacon."

The dog backed up, looked at Kory, and then spun a circle before he disappeared into the bedroom. *Odd.* Kory's gut clenched the way it always did when she was examining a patient and instinct told her to take a closer look. For the first time in years, she didn't want to pursue her instinct. But four agonizing steps later, she was inside the bedroom.

Smith sat on the bed beside Dad. It wasn't like him to sleep in. Maybe he drank more than she realized at the reception.

"Hey, you two. Time for breakfast." The words felt tacky in her mouth, and the hair on the back of her neck stood on end.

Dad's hand trembled, but his head didn't turn.

Shit. "Dad?" She jumped toward him. One good look was all it took for her to grab the bedside phone. "Hang in there, Dad. You're having a stroke. Mom," she called over her shoulder as she dialed.

"911. What's your emergency?"

Kory rattled off the details with surprising detachment. Stroke. Right-sided weakness, unable to talk. By the time she hung up the phone, her mother was screaming at her side.

"Ken! Oh my God! Ken!" And then she looked at Kory. "Do something."

But there wasn't anything she could do except make sure he stayed breathing—make sure she stayed breathing, too. "He's going to be okay," she said, gathering his lifeless hand in her hand and staring hard into his wide eyes. "Paramedics are on their way."

• • •

Will walked into the meeting room at Harmony Falls Elder Care and twenty women went silent.

"Ladies," Will said, flashing a smile around the packed room. "Thank you for meeting with me." He sat in the empty chair at the head of the table and removed his father's Montblanc pen from his inside breast pocket, setting it gently atop the legal pad with the engraving facing up. "Valley Hospital System, which owns Valley Hospital in Rileyville, has recently purchased two smaller hospitals in the surrounding community, and now, they want to purchase this independently owned nursing home from my family. Their intention is to close the nursing home, transfer the patients and current employees to their hospital-owned nursing homes in Rileyville, and build a free-standing, Valley Hospital-affiliated urgent care in this space. Of course, you all probably know this by now, because nothing is a secret in Harmony Falls." A few women chuckled while others nodded. "If you've attended any of the town hall meetings, you also know the majority is in favor of the deal because it means not having to drive to Rileyville for things like broken bones anymore. But the deal's not done until all terms are agreed upon, including your terms. So…" he tapped his fingers on the pen "…shall we get started?"

The moratorium on talking broken, noise exploded until their voices amounted to nothing more than the buzz of a swarm of mosquitos. He held up his hands. "Bev, let's start with you."

The woman to his right pinched at her brightly colored scrub top, pulling it away from her belly. "I talked to Joe about this. He said he learned a lot about rights from the electrician's union. Said we need to make sure our service here counts toward retirement credits there."

Will nodded and scribbled the request on the legal pad. "Sounds reasonable. Who has the most seniority?"

"Gerty. Right?" Bev asked as she leaned forward and looked down the long table.

"Twenty years," Gertrude said, nodding.

Bev kept talking, but seeing the woman who unceremoniously interrupted last night's kiss with Kory, left Will jostled for a second or two. If she hadn't walked in, how far would things have gone?

The sensible majority in his brain snatched control, shoving him back into the present. "I'm sorry, Bev. Can you repeat that?"

"I said, will they pay for parking in one of those garages, or will we have to? I think they should."

One after the other, the women spoke in surprisingly efficient order, while Will short-handed everything. As he crossed the T's in "Troutman," Janelle spoke up. "We don't have dental here. We'd like dental."

Will nodded. "I would be surprised if it's not part of the benefits package for a big hospital system, but I'll verify."

"Back to the idea of our years here counting," Gertrude said. "Can you make that across the board, not just for retirement? I'd hate to be stuck with the worst shifts because they look at me as low-woman on the totem pole."

Will didn't see how that would work. Existing staff wouldn't be happy to give up prime shifts to newcomers, but he wrote it down anyway, and by the time the hour ended, he'd filled four legal-sized pages with his chicken scratch.

On his way out of the meeting room, Fran grabbed his arm. "Thank you."

"I haven't done anything yet. Hold that thought for when I strike a decent deal." He thought to pat the nursing home director's hand but instead he offered an awkward smile.

"What do you mean you haven't done anything? We all know your family is keeping this place fully staffed even though it's never been a moneymaker, and you're losing a ton of money every day it stays open. You could've closed it when Dr. Render retired. Lots of people say that."

He shook his head. "Don't believe everything you hear, Fran."

"I don't have to. I can form my own opinions. I know this business. I've seen the books. So thank you." She squeezed his arm.

Something tickled his Adam's apple until he coughed. If she knew how tenuous this deal was, she wouldn't be praising him. Valley Hospital System had done an excellent job of enticing the Mitchells and leading them on. Lately, his gut told him the end result of this back and forth wasn't going to be good. In that case, keeping the home fully staffed without a way to recoup the financial loss wasn't heroic—it was stupid. At least that's what his mother would say.

Fran walked ahead down the wide hallway's peeling laminate floors, and then stopped to chat with Gertrude. The women smiled brightly as he passed them. No doubt, they'd be talking about him as soon as he was beyond earshot. Between the buyout and the kiss Gertrude witnessed last night, there was quite a bit to say.

Will slipped his right hand beneath his suit coat to rub the hotspot of nerves on his left side. He hated to think people were talking about him, especially when the talk revolved around anything other than his personal and professional successes, but he couldn't change what he did in that coat room, and he couldn't deny Fran's statements about the dire predicament this home was in. His mother was right; it was the sole black mark in the Mitchell family business portfolio. It was the sole black mark on him.

Let them talk, he thought. He had bigger worries.

Without Valley Hospital System, Will couldn't stop the chronically under-filled nursing home from bleeding money. Hell, he couldn't even slow the bleeding without some of these women becoming unemployed. And then there was patient care. A week ago, he'd deepened the debt in order to get Lance Palmer to agree to take on the medical directorship left vacant by Dr. Render's retirement. Will was paying double for half the services, because running a failing nursing home until it was bulldozed in favor of an urgent care so Mitchell Company, Inc. could bank the hospital's payout and claim all assets profitable again wasn't high on any doctor's career achievement list.

He peeked into rundown rooms as he walked, nodding to the few coherent patients that remained. It sucked. It really sucked. Making sure everyone was happy was an impossible job.

"Have a good day, Mr. Mitchell," Bess said, smiling at him overtop the reception desk.

"You, too," he answered as he punched in the code to exit the building.

An ambulance screamed down Main Street, heading out of town toward Rileyville. He wondered whom the unlucky man or woman was, and then wondered if the injury was something that could be treated in a state-of-the-art urgent care. If so, he'd hear about it. Justin's mayoral opponent Frank Cleed and his crew of supporters would be squawking about all the time the Mitchells were wasting, waiting on the perfect deal.

Well, they could bring it on. If there was one thing Will thrived on, it was competition.

• • •

Kory stared at the time, glowing larger than life on her phone screen, and then returned her gaze to the empty holding room, where she waited for her father to return from a CT scan. She missed her flight, and she couldn't reschedule until he was stable. Her program director at the rehab center understood, but it brought little comfort. Kory knew too much about stroke to feel anything other than distinct fear.

Aside from concern for her father's basic survival, she was worried about the stroke extending and the hemiparesis being permanent. He was a fifty-year-old roofer, for crying out loud. She couldn't imagine him never regaining normal function. He'd rather be dead.

Her insides twisted until she thought she might throw up.

"Aunt Jeanie's on her way." Mom clutched the looped handles of her purse with both hands as she walked into the room. The gesture wasn't enough to stop her hands from visibly shaking.

"There's really no reason for her to rush over here," Kory said. "There's nothing she can do…"

"When she gets here, you can go."

Kory blinked. "I'm not going until…well, until I say I'm going." Usually, Kory was grateful for her parents' near-overzealous support of her medical career. They'd pushed her and sacrificed so she could attend university and medical school in Chicago, and when she'd decided to stay there after initial training was complete, they'd never tried to guilt her into coming back or even visiting often; but honestly, not expecting her to stay and advocate for her father, who was having a stroke, when she was nearly an expert on the subject? It was kind of ridiculous.

"Thank you."

And frustrating.

"Don't thank me. It's not some favor I'm doing you. He's my dad. I'm staying."

A clang from the hall announced his return before the foot-end of the gurney came into view.

Her mother rushed to his good side, gripping his hand, while Kory locked eyes on the doctor entering the room behind him.

"So?" she asked.

"Large right-sided middle cerebral artery infarct."

Shit. Kory closed her eyes, taking a moment to process what she already suspected.

"What's that mean?" Mom asked.

"He had a stroke." It was a flip answer, but it was also the easiest answer.

"Didn't we already know that?"

"We assumed that, but now we have confirmation." Kory opened her mouth and dragged in a shallow breath. "We also know it was severe."

"Severe?" Tears pooled in Mom's eyes, and Kory fought a fresh wave of panic. "But he'll get better won't he?"

"Better is a relative term." Honest to God, she never thought she'd see the day when she wished she wasn't a doctor.

"We're going to do everything we can while he's under our care, Mrs. Flemming."

Kory glanced at the doctor who had a better bedside manner than she did. He was leaving out just enough to give her mother hope. Early on in her training, Kory decided compassion like that was a God-given talent—one she didn't have. Oh, she felt sorry for people, but the medical puzzle and its ultimate solution kept her bothered more than the patient's or their loved ones' emotional states. Restoring a person's healthy, functioning body had to take precedent over feelings.

"How long will he be here?" Mom asked as she stroked her husband's crippled hand.

"It's hard to say," the friendly doctor said. "Maybe one to two weeks."

"Do you hear that, honey? You get a two-week vacation from those rooftops." Her unconvincing chuckle echoed in the barren room. "I'm always on him to take a vacation," she said, looking from the doctor to Kory. "Now he can't argue."

But he tried, in that gravelly, garbled speech of a stroke patient that Kory had come to know all too well. She caught a few recognizable words in the mix. Crew. Bills. Farm. The harder he tried to be heard, the more the left side of his face drooped.

Kory closed her eyes as sadness seeped into every pore. She roughed palms over her face and wondered where the doctor's ridiculous optimism was now.

A moment later it returned.

"Vacations are good, Mr. Flemming."

Kory opened her eyes and glared at the man. He was an idiot, dosing out false hope instead of information the family could use to prepare for what laid ahead.

"It's not a vacation," she said. "He'll be here for two weeks, and then he'll be discharged to a nursing home for rehabilitation. He'll be in the nursing home indefinitely."

Mom turned her head and gaped at Kory. She blinked a few times, and then she looked at the male doctor, as if she needed confirmation. "Is that correct?"

Kory ground her molars so hard her ears popped.

"That is correct," the doctor said. "But I don't want you to worry about it right now. Let's focus on what's going on here."

Kory saw tears in her mother's eyes, and she looked away to her father who was once again trying to speak. "He's too young for a nursing home," she said.

Any annoyance Kory felt over her facts being double-checked faded as memories of last night's family dance filtered in. She would've danced longer and laughed louder if she'd known it might never happen again. She couldn't remember ever feeling so hopeless. His life would never be the same. The stark truth pushed her stomach into her throat.

"Nursing homes serve people of all ages," the doctor said. "And when we get to that point, Rileyville has some of the best in the area." He nodded and stepped backward, like he was ready to leave.

Figured. Toss the family some tidbit of hope and move on—just when they were starting to fall apart under the weight of so many unanswered questions.

Kory stepped forward. "For the record, my father will go to Harmony Elder Care."

"He can't," Mom said, glancing over her shoulder.

"What do you mean he can't? You can't take care of him yourself. He's too big, and in-home care is too expensive, and…"

"Harmony Elder Care is closed to new admissions."

Kory looked at the retreating doctor, who was now half in and half out of the doorway. She knew he had other patients to see. Heck, how many times had she done something similar, hurrying things along so she didn't get swept up in an extra thirty minutes of emotional conversation? And because she'd been on the other side, she wasn't going to let him leave…yet.

"Are they at capacity?" she asked incredulously. It was a rundown, private nursing home in a rural location where the county home had more than enough room for the bulk of the area's low-income patients. There had to be a single bed available at Harmony Elder Care.

"Not exactly. As far as I know, they're preparing to shut down."

Kory shook her head. "That can't be right." Sure, the home wasn't the most state-of-the-art or financially sound, but it was Mitchell-owned, and the Mitchells didn't let things shut down.

The doctor took one more step back, and looked down the hall. Another detachment technique Kory was familiar with. "Maybe something's changed," he said. "I'll ask our social worker."

And he would. Only Kory knew he wasn't going to dash down that hall and find the woman right away.

Part of her wanted to call him on it, but she kept her mouth shut. She had no use for him anymore. He could ask his social worker in his own good time. Kory would go straight to the source.

• • •

Will pinched the bridge of his nose as he listened to Lou Sullivan complain about noise from the lumber mill that the Mitchells owned on Rural Route Five scaring water fowl from his land.

"I'll see what I can do," he said, knowing he wasn't going to put much effort behind the statement. Honestly, he had bigger worries now that Valley Hospital System had digested the nurses' and aides' benefit requests and made it clear they weren't going to let the terms be named.

Fortunately, the half-hearted statement placated Lou as usual, and Will hung up the phone, eager to return to serious business. He hit the play button on his Bose remote and sighed as strains of Puccini fought against the worry, trying to drown out his depressing thoughts. But it was going to take more than opera to fix this mess.

Georgiana appeared in the doorway. Her eyes were wide, and her lips curved down. Normally, his secretary was the picture of stoicism.

This day wasn't going to get any better, was it?

"Did you hear about Ken Flemming?" she asked.

The last name caused an immediate, blinding headache. "No."

"They had to take him by ambulance to Rileyville. He had a stroke. I guess it's pretty bad."

Will remembered the ambulance he'd seen racing past the nursing home. He closed his eyes on an inhale.

"Should I send something? Flowers maybe?"

He nodded as he opened his eyes. "Yes, please." Georgiana started to back away, but he stopped her with his voice. "Did, uh, is, uh, Kory still in town?" He closed his eyes briefly again, because his reason for asking was incredibly shallow considering her father's stroke.

"Yep. Joyce said the whole family's over at the hospital."

For a split second, he thought about delivering the flowers in person, bolstered by the news that Kory was here, but no matter what happened between them at the reception, seeing him wasn't going to magically brighten her day.

"Thanks, Georgiana," he said. "That'll be all." And he meant it.

The flowers would serve as both a peace offering and a get-well wish. Will had enough difficulties to manage without inserting himself into whatever was happening at the hospital.

CHAPTER FOUR

"I don't need you to turn around and drive home, Alice. I need to talk to Justin." Kory dropped her head to the steering wheel of her father's pick-up truck and fought a wave of guilt for calling to dump a load of junk all over her best friend's honeymoon.

Alice huffed. "Fine, but I'm still coming home."

"No." But Kory was pretty sure the word evaporated into thin air.

She waited impatiently, tapping her foot at the sounds of rustling on the other end. Distracted, she gazed out the windshield at the hospital entrance. She had a fellowship to finish, research projects in the works, and a career to return to, but none of that seemed important now that she also had a father who was struggling after a major stroke and a mother who was beside herself with worry.

"Hey, Kory. I'm sorry to hear about your father. What can I do to help?"

"Thanks, Justin. You can start by telling me why Harmony Elder Care is closed to admissions." Eventually, she would have to return to Chicago, and it would be easier to do so knowing she'd eased her parents' burden at least a smidge.

"I'm sure you've heard Valley Hospital System is interested in purchasing the property, and building an urgent care. The back and forth has been going on for a few months now, but from what Will tells me, a deal is close, hence no new admissions."

Will. God, he was the last person she wanted to deal with now. Well, whatever. She'd work around him, and concentrate on what really mattered. Her parents.

"I need you to make an exception, Justin. You know my mother doesn't drive since her seizures. How is she going to get to Rileyville every day to see my dad when I'm not here to drive her?"

"We can help. Alice can coordinate some sort of driving schedule."

"Every day? Indefinitely? And what about the dogs? She'd need to be brought back a couple times a day to tend to them, unless a schedule could be made for their care. It's too much to expect from people. It would be so much easier if you just let him come to Harmony until we see how his recovery progresses. The place is still staffed, isn't it?"

"Yes, but…"

"Then, what's one more person? If he doesn't get better by the time the home closes, then…" her throat contracted "…I'll figure something out, but for the time being, having him close to home is the best thing for him and my mom."

She was begging, wasn't she? How many times had she weathered the pleas of a patient's family, knowing they were asking for a miracle? Being on the opposite end was sobering.

"Okay." Her relief was cut short when he added, "But Kory, I can't make any promises. I'll have to talk to Will first."

If Will screwed this up for her…

"Thank you, Justin. I'm sorry to dump this on you during your honeymoon, but I appreciate the help. If you could keep me updated, that'd be great."

Long after she ended the call, Kory sat in the truck, processing everything, avoiding the strange turn her life had taken. To think she'd come home for a wedding, the ultimate celebration, and now she had a gut-wrenching choice to make: take an official leave of absence from fellowship, delaying completion and boards, which would risk the dream job she had waiting for her in Chicago, or let someone else support her parents and oversee her father's care. She'd always been focused and determined when it came to her academic and professional goals, but she couldn't imagine returning to Chicago to treat other stroke patients when her father was in need of the same treatment here.

With a sigh, she dropped her head to the steering wheel and closed her eyes, hoping Justin could convince Will one more patient didn't matter.

•••

"No." Will's jaw ticked as he said the word that made him sound like a heartless bastard.

"What do you mean no? What's one more person?" Justin asked.

"One more person is a breach in Lance Palmer's contract, and I have no doubt he'll walk, leaving us without a medical director. Do you know how hard it was to find Dr. Render's replacement? It was damn near impossible. If Lance walks, I guarantee you our mother will insist the home be closed—deal or no deal with Valley. As much as I want to help the Flemmings, I can't sacrifice the people already here for them. Ken can get great care in Rileyville."

It was the truth. It all made sense. But Will's heart pinched anyway.

"Carole can't drive, and those dogs need somebody checking on them throughout the day," Justin said. He all but pleaded his case.

Of course Will's bleeding-heart, politician brother had the luxury of championing the underdog. With the company resting squarely on Will's shoulders, he was once again the bad guy, seemingly putting business first.

Will exhaled. "Then I'll drive Carole to Rileyville every day if I have to, and I'll let the dogs out while she's there, but that's all I can do."

Three hours later, Will still felt like a jerk. He imagined Kory hearing the news that he wouldn't allow her father to be admitted to Harmony Elder Care, and he couldn't accept her going back to thinking he was a jerk. So he called Lance, looking for a miracle—or at least someone to share the burden of being the bad guy.

"What's his condition? How long are we talking here?"

"I don't know," Will answered honestly. He jumped the gun with this phone call, which was unlike him. Normally, he didn't initiate a call like this without having all the information he needed to make a persuasive case. He was definitely off his game, and had been since that damn wedding reception.

"Well, you need to know. The current patients are easily managed. I can't run a private practice that's forty-five minutes away and oversee a nursing home if you're going to be adding a complex case. I can't. I refuse. If he's in bad shape and you bring him in, you're going to need to find a new medical director."

Will was afraid of that. Worse yet, there was no relief in having someone to share the burden of being the bad guy. When it came down to it, Will knew Kory would blame him.

• • •

Five days had passed since Kory's father's stroke, and she was running out of time and apparently options. Justin's call earlier that morning revealed Lance Palmer refused the admission. It was an attempt to close the door on Harmony Elder Care. But as long as Kory had her arm in the crack, she still had a shot at getting her father in—even if that shot made her queasy.

Kory didn't want to face Will, not after the stupid lapse of judgment she'd suffered at Alice's wedding, but now was not the time to let high school histrionics dictate her next move. Despite the queasiness, Kory held her head high as she walked into the Mitchell Company, Inc. reception area. As the daughter of the town roofer and retired librarian, she'd never had cause or power to be inside the Mitchell family business compound. It was mildly intimidating.

"Hi," Georgiana said, smiling. "How's your dad?"

Kory answered that question on an average of ten times a day. "He's been better." She had stopped giving details after the second day. Everyone seemed to know the depressing truth anyway.

"I'm so sorry. I still smile when I remember how he squeezed in my little ole gutter repair between the Parrishes and Mitchells' new roofs after that big storm—such a sweetheart! And if the number of prayer lists I hear he's on has anything to do with it, he'll be up and around in no time."

Georgiana was sincere and sweet, but sadly mistaken. A man who suffered a large middle cerebral artery infarct wasn't going to be up and around soon. But Kory wasn't going to say that, especially not to a woman who saw the good in everything and everybody.

Kory inhaled and exhaled a small smile. "Thanks. Is Will in?"

Georgiana nodded. "But, uh, he had a call earlier. Wait here a minute, and I'll see if he's free."

Kory watched the woman disappear into the room behind her. When the door closed, she contemplated walking out. She did not want to be here. She most certainly did not want to enter that room and close the door. Her face flushed on memories of their kiss, but she wasn't here for a repeat performance. She was here for a showdown. Fighting with Will was the last thing she wanted. But this wasn't about what she wanted. This was about her parents, two people who had always put Kory's wants and needs first.

It was time to return the favor. Georgiana reappeared, and Kory's nerves reached a rapid boil. "You can go in." She lifted her purse by the strap off the back of her desk chair. "I'm going to grab some lunch. Probably won't be back before you leave, so good luck to your dad, and tell your mom I'm here if she needs anything."

Kory nodded and tried to swallow down the nervous bubble. She wished she could make Georgiana stay, because the idea of walking into Will's office and closing the door was a bit more manageable if his secretary was right outside. And that was ridiculous. Kory put one foot in front of the other until she gripped the knob with sweaty hands. *This is about Dad. Not you. Not Will.*

She pushed into the room.

Tense opera music filled the air. Will was standing with his back to her, his body facing the window that overlooked the pond. He turned his head in her direction, and when their eyes met, awareness of what transpired between them the last time they'd shared a closed-off room heated her skin and restricted her chest.

He looked away first, facing the window again, and shoved his hands into his dress pants pockets. A light blue dress shirt covered his back, stretching across his broad shoulders. Kory could see those shoulders rising and falling. He looked bigger, more formidable, certainly less relaxed than the last time she saw him. She struggled to contain the attraction building inside of her, causing her feet to step toward him and her palms to crave the feel of him.

The rough sound of him clearing his throat rose over the melancholy music and halted her progress.

"My hands are tied. There's nothing I can do." He couldn't even look at her when he said it.

The words put an end to her attraction. "Can you at least look me in the eyes when you tell me business is more important than people?" she asked.

He looked at her, shoulders back, chin lifted, eyes bleak. "The success of a business ensures the success of the people."

Kory sneered. "This isn't an economics lecture, but hey, whatever helps you sleep."

He exhaled, deflating a bit, and when his head bowed, she hardened her muscles against the onslaught of pity. She didn't want a soft spot for Will Mitchell when she was trying to beat him at his own game. She didn't. But...

"I tried, Kory. I swear. I asked Lance. When he heard your father's prognosis, he said no way."

"What kind of doctor stands in the way of what's best for a patient? What kind of man hires a doctor like that?"

"A man who didn't have any other options. There's not many doctors who'd sign up to run a failing nursing home in a struggling small town." He righted his posture, and stared at her hard enough to make her avert her eyes to the window behind him. The sky was gray and thick with clouds. The scene was as fitting as the music, building to a crescendo. "I certainly didn't see your application cross my desk," he continued. "But then it's not nearly as *challenging* as a flashy Chicago rehab hospital, is it?"

She flinched. The truth hurt. She couldn't imagine how desperate she'd have to be to build a career in Harmony Falls, or if what she would build could even be called a career. That probably said more about her than she cared to consider, so she deflected his personal attack. "Don't make this about me."

He stepped toward her. "Then whom should I make it about? Your father? Isn't he going to get arguably better care in Rileyville at a newer, bigger facility?"

She'd asked herself the same question, and had tried to convince both her parents of the same thing. Rileyville could offer more, but her parents had been adamant.

"He doesn't want to be there. He wants to be here. He wants to be home near my mother and the rest of his family and friends."

"I understand that, but—"

"Do you? I don't think you do. Because if you did, you'd be trying harder to keep that home up and running."

"So this is about me and my shortcomings as a business man?"

"Maybe."

He grunted and shoved his hands deeper into his pockets. "You don't know what you're talking about."

She laughed. "After the training I've had, I could run that place into the black with my eyes closed."

And just like that, the air wooshed from the room.

"Are you proposing a challenge?"

Of course she wasn't. Of course he would think she was. Of course everything was out of control.

She pressed a palm to her overheated cheek and inhaled, annoyed by the situation, annoyed by her surroundings. "You know I can't do that."

"Why not?"

"Because I have a fellowship to finish and a job waiting for me in Chicago and…"

"We all have priorities." The intensity of his gaze made her want to smack him.

What was he insinuating? That her career was more of a priority than her father regaining use of his body? If that were the case, she'd be no better than Will, putting business before people.

Kory scoffed. This was so not the same.

"I shouldn't have come. It's obvious there's no compromise here." She spun around on the cork heels of her sandals and stalked to the door.

"If you change your mind, you know where to find me."

There wasn't a chance in hell that was going to happen.

• • •

Will slumped into his leather desk chair and blasted air across his loose lips just in time for Puccini's "Nessun dorma" to end. A heavy, fitting silence echoed in the empty office.

What was that? Kory came to him for help, and he offered her a job—more like dangled one in front of her face, and not because she needed one, but because he supposed she was desperate enough to consider it. In all honesty, he was the desperate one, wasn't he?

He opened the email from Chris Kent at Valley, re-reading the third sentence: *We're going to have to postpone the purchase indefinitely.* Nothing before or after those words mattered. His mother was going to be livid. Without the Valley Hospital System deal, Will had two options. He could close the home effective immediately, which would no doubt make his mother happy and at least cap the mounting debt. It would also make a dozen residents homeless and a complete nursing home staff jobless. Or, he could fight his mother, because contrary to what Kory thought of him, he didn't like putting business first. If he could find a doctor to replace Lance, one with a vested interest in the impossible task of making Harmony Elder Care a success, he might be able to convince his mother to keep the home off the "for sale" list.

Too bad that doctor just walked out of his office, undoubtedly never to return.

CHAPTER FIVE

Her mother blinked at Kory from overtop the rim of her coffee cup. "I appreciate you being here. I do, but you need to go back to Chicago, before everything you've worked so hard for gets messed up. Your dreams are there."

No matter how sweetly Mom managed to assemble and say the words, they stung, making it feel like Kory had overstayed her welcome, again. It happened every time she was home, and this time, it was wearing her thin.

Kory picked a blueberry out of the top of her muffin and licked the sweet goo from her fingertip. "Chicago's not going anywhere."

"Won't they get mad?"

"My dad just had a major stroke. I'm entitled to get things in order. They understand." And after meeting with Will Mitchell, Kory understood getting things in order wasn't going to be easy.

Mom nodded and sipped from her cup again. Kory dug another blueberry out of the muffin. It wasn't that she always ate so painstakingly slow. On the contrary, she normally couldn't remember what she ate and when she even ate it. But sitting in the hospital cafeteria, picking blueberries out of her muffin was one way to prolong the return to her father's room—not that she didn't want to see him. It was just hard to see him like that and not want to take over his care, tell everyone how everything should be done. She'd already made a not-so-nice name for herself with the nursing staff.

"The Manions are going to take Smith and Wesson."

Kory looked up from her mutilated muffin. "Take them where?"

"Take them in. They have all those acres, and Selma works from home. It will be good for them."

"You're giving away the dogs?" Kory gaped.

"I don't know what else to do. I need to be here, and they're not used to being home alone. It seems like a reasonable solution."

Well, shoot. Kory flattened palms against the table and inhaled. As if things didn't suck enough already. She exhaled and tipped her face to the ceiling. Her father would be devastated if he knew they were even having this discussion. Smith and Wesson were his girls—maybe more so than Kory was. The trio never missed a hunting season.

"It won't be forever. As soon as he's well enough to come home, I'll bring them back." Mom placed her crinkled napkin on her empty plate and stood. "We should get going. You ready?"

No. Kory wasn't ready. She wasn't ready to return to the room where her father couldn't move freely. She wasn't ready to give the dogs away. She wasn't ready to resume life in Chicago, where she was some gifted doctor on the cusp of a fast-paced, enviable career. Not when everything here was falling apart. There had to be something more she could do.

Will. A fuzzy image of his smug face popped into her head as his challenge-turned-job-offer rang in her ears. He couldn't want her to work for him anymore than she wanted to work for him, but she couldn't completely ignore the option.

"How about you go up?" Kory offered a reassuring smile. "I'll stay here, finish my muffin, and then head home to let out the dogs."

"Oh, that sounds like a good idea. In fact, I wish you would stay there." Mom patted her shoulder. "Aunt Jeannie is heading over after work, and she can bring me back later tonight. You could use the quiet time to get your return flight in order." She kissed Kory on the crown of the head. "You've worked so hard to get where you are. I hate to see you lose ground because of this. Daddy doesn't want you sitting around wringing your hands like me when you can be finishing up fellowship and starting that fancy job." She sniffed and kissed Kory again. Her next words were whispered. "We're so very proud of you."

Kory had no doubt her mother was crying. She reached up and set her hand on top of her mother's, squeezing. "I know you are." That pride had been propelling Kory away from Harmony Falls in the shape of academic camps and elite higher education for as long as she could remember, but sometimes that pride felt like a noose around her neck.

"Then it's settled. You go. There's no reason for your future to suffer."

As much as Kory wished she was driven enough to hop a flight to Chicago and leave all of this turmoil behind, it didn't feel like the right thing to do. But what was the right thing to do?

Kory wrapped the barely eaten muffin in a napkin as she watched her mother walk away. Mom thought the rational thing for Kory to do was stay through the end of the week and leave with her father stable and on track for discharge to a nursing home. But rational didn't feel *right*. Kory squeezed the wrapped muffin until it crumbled in her hand. She couldn't imagine her mother sleeping alone in the big farmhouse—without the dogs even.

An impossible brick wall stood between Kory and Chicago. Leaving at any time before her father was well enough to return home meant turning her back on the two people who loved her most while they suffered. She couldn't do it.

Not when there was something she could do to make things better.

• • •

Will maintained the inhuman pace all the way to the five-mile marker. That was when he was finally too exhausted to think. Without his brain pumping out a never-ending list of negative repercussions as a result of the failed nursing home sale, all that remained was the crunch of trail mulch under his feet. This was what he'd come in search of. Peace.

He slowed down and turned around at the bridge, jogging back the way he came, noting each drop of sweat as it slipped down his cheek and pooled at the dip in his neck. It was an oddly satisfying state. Of course, the closer he got to the end of the trail, the more his brain anticipated the end of the run, and stressful thinking crept in. He was going to have to tell his mother soon. If she insisted on selling the nursing home on the open market, Will was going to challenge her. This wasn't just about money. If they were going to sell, he wanted the property to remain useful to the majority of Harmony Falls residents. Few people would benefit from another piece of prime property outfitted with a diesel pump and parking for two-dozen eighteen-wheelers. And he wanted new job opportunities for the women who would be unemployed by the sale. It was a lot to ask.

Slowing his pace further when he reached the trail welcome sign and the empty dirt parking lot beyond, Will lifted the hem of his shirt and swiped it across his soaking forehead. Grime marred the white T. He could feel sweat dripping down his neck, so he ripped off the shirt and wiped his head and shoulders, and then hung the garment around his neck. The summer breeze felt good and his house was only a few yards away. Will slowed to a walk, hands on hips, face tipped to the clear blue sky. He had no idea what was going to happen, but something had to give. He didn't want to be passing out pink slips to women whose paychecks were the only thing putting food on their tables.

Cutting across a patch of sprawling crabgrass, he headed for his house, wanting nothing more than a cold shower followed by an even colder beer. Instead, he found Ken Flemming's pick-up truck idling in the driveway and Kory behind the wheel. Curiosity picked up the hairs on his damp skin. She was the last person he'd ever expect to find here.

The driver's side window was down, and her elbow propped on the door. She glanced at him as he walked up the driveway, but then she looked away and rubbed the left side of her face in her hand.

"Hey," he managed, despite a combination of lingering breathlessness from the run and pure shock at seeing her.

The engine rumbled. She gripped the steering wheel with both hands and stared straight ahead. He had the feeling she was seconds away from gunning it into reverse and driving away.

"Is everything okay?" he asked, hoping her father's condition hadn't worsened.

"What if I did stay…in Harmony Falls…for a little bit?" Her knuckles turned white. "Would you hire me, admit my dad, and let me run the place?"

Will opened his mouth to breathe, lifted the edge of the T-shirt hanging around his neck, and took another swipe at his face, still finding it hard to believe she was here when she'd walked out of his office so definitively the other day. Why the change of heart?

She *might* stay. For a *little bit*. "There's a lot of ambiguity in those words," he finally said.

"Stop it, Will." She looked at him, and her gaze flashed from his face down to his bare chest and back up. That simple glance had him swiping at his face again to quell the fresh rush of heat.

She stayed quiet, staring at him with an open mouth, letting whatever was lingering between them fester until he felt like maybe he should put on his shirt—or kiss her again, which was completely inappropriate considering the conversation.

She blinked, gave her head a subtle shake, and looked away again. "Don't give me a hard time right now."

"I'm not. I'm just trying to figure out what this really means."

"If *you* hiring *me* will get my father into Harmony Elder Care, then hire me. That's as plain as I can make it."

"Temporarily? Is that until he's well enough to return home?"

Her frown deepened. "Ideally."

"How long will that take?"

"I don't know."

"What about Chicago?"

She paused before answering. "It will still be there."

Will saw the convulsion of her throat, the way she reached up with one shaky hand to calm the movement. He'd heard Kory's medical career was so bright it was damn near blinding. She was making one hell of a sacrifice for her father, and Will found her willingness to do so even more impressive than the career she was walking away from. *Temporarily*, he reminded himself. As soon as her father was better, she'd be gone.

Was it wrong for Will to hope she would stay long enough to save his ass, too? If she was as good as everyone said, maybe she could get the home back in the black, and then hiring someone new wouldn't be such a problem. Maybe. Hopefully. What else could he do?

"Okay," he said, committing to the only plan that gave him any sense of hope.

She looked at him, her brows high on her forehead. "Okay? Just like that? I thought you'd make me beg."

He coughed an awkward laugh as a bolt of lust sliced through him. He should've thought this through—all the way through. Working with Kory would be complicated. They shared a penchant for competition...and one hell of a kiss.

"This isn't going to be easy," he said.

"I know that." Her brows dropped, twisting together at the top of her nose, and her mouth frowned. "Believe me. None of this is easy, but staying here, helping him, it's the right thing to do."

Confidence shone on her face, smoothing the worry lines and sparkling in her green eyes. She might be ambivalent about the decision to stay in Harmony Falls, but he got the sense it wasn't because she couldn't handle the job she was proposing to do. He sure hoped she could handle it. This was the most unconventional job interview he'd ever conducted. They hadn't even talked salary, never mind Kory's experience. Had she ever worked in elder care before?

Will would have asked if this wasn't his only shot to save the nursing home. She'd been enough of a quick study in high school to step in and write a Model U.N. position paper that nearly sent her to the U.N. conference in his place. If she lacked practical experience where nursing homes were concerned, hopefully she was still a fast learner. Will pushed any concerns aside and said, "I'll call Lance."

"I can start tomorrow."

He bet she could. If she were half as driven and determined as he suspected, she'd be up all night planning a whole list of things she wanted to change—or maybe just cursing the allegiance to her father that had brought her straight to Will.

This isn't going to be easy. They were his words. Maybe he should slow things down.

"Tomorrow is Saturday." He smiled. "But we can do the paperwork for hire. Come by my office around ten. And if you change your mind before then, so be it. I won't hold it against you."

She inhaled and exhaled, her breath fluttering a strand of copper hair skirting her cheek, and then she tipped her head and narrowed her eyes. The look was more speculation than challenge. "This is weird."

"What's weird?"

"Us working together."

After the kiss in the coat closet and the chemistry between them, he wasn't sure he'd call anything they did together weird, exactly. He stepped toward the truck and slid his hand to the window ledge, curling his fingers around the vinyl, watching her lips part to breathe. "Maybe it's not weird at all. Maybe it's meant to be."

She blinked, closed her mouth and yanked the gearshift. "I'll see you tomorrow at ten."

His hand slipped off the door as the car rolled backward. He watched her take the narrow road faster than necessary and wondered if it felt to Kory like she was fleeing as much as it looked like she was. Convoluted thoughts. Complicated situations. He was ready for that beer, because tomorrow he was going to have to face his mother, tell her about this turn of events, and then he was going to have to face Kory again, knowing all he wanted was to get her alone. And not so they could talk about high school antics, sick parents, or nursing homes. In fact, for what he had in mind, they didn't need to talk at all.

CHAPTER SIX

Kory sat on the front stoop watching the dogs wrestle in the front yard drenched in the orange glow of setting sun. She glanced down the dirt road, wishing Alice was just a rocky five-minute walk away, but the house at the end of the street was empty. Then she remembered that even if Alice weren't hundreds of miles away on her honeymoon, she wouldn't be *there*. She lived with her husband on the other side of town. How things changed…

Normally, at this time of night, her father would be pulling into the drive after a long day of work, and her mother would be in the kitchen, the dogs clamoring for scraps at her feet. But that wouldn't be happening tonight—or anytime soon.

The breath Kory let out pushed apart her lips and mixed with humid evening air. A bird squawked in the distance. Smith yelped, and Wesson bolted. Both dogs took off around the side of the house. Kory didn't move, even when a mosquito landed on her hand above her wrist. She absently watched its body grow fat and red as her thoughts wandered. She'd been home exactly ten days, and already her life was unrecognizable. She didn't even feel like the same person. Gone was her single-minded pursuit of professional success. And while that wasn't a bad thing, considering her father's heart-wrenching condition, it was a scary thing. Who would she be without the regimented schedule that kept her from the chaos that caused people to make poor decisions?

Aunt Jeannie's car rattled on the dirt road, bringing Kory to her feet. She scratched at the spot where the mosquito had been— even though it wasn't itchy. It gave her something to do with her nervous hands. A few hours ago, Will said working for him wasn't going to be easy. Well, she knew something that might be even harder…telling her mother she was staying in Harmony Falls.

"Hi, Baby," Aunt Jeannie called out her open window, waving her left hand, jingling an armful of bangle bracelets. "Can't stay. Uncle Milt has poker, but love, love, love you!" She punctuated each love with the smack of her hand to her lips.

Kory opened her left hand and caught the last blown kiss, like she'd been doing for decades, and when she touched the same hand to her lips to blow a kiss back, she smiled. Next to Alice, Aunt Jeannie was the most exuberant person Kory knew. She'd forgotten how nice it was to be around people who smiled more than they scowled.

Aunt Jeannie's baby sister, on the other hand, shuffled around the front of the car looking tired and old. It was further confirmation Kory was right to delay her return to Chicago until things were taken care of here, but that didn't make the conversation she was about to have any easier. Mom had made it clear she wanted Kory to return to Chicago. The urging was wrapped in the context of pride, but it seemed misplaced. Why weren't they like most parents, thrilled to have their child home—especially their only child?

Memories rushed in, dragging Kory's exhales back into her chest. She remembered all the times her mother and father pushed her away to camps and conferences in the name of achievement. She'd used their excitement over her achievements to compensate for the sadness she'd felt at being pushed away. Kory shook her head as she watched her mother pause and wave to Aunt Jeannie. It was one thing for them to encourage her absence when she'd been a fourteen-year-old questioning whether or not she wanted to spend the summer abroad, but after her father's stroke? It didn't make sense.

The dogs returned, tumbling in the green space at Kory's feet.

A few yips and growls, and Mom sighed. "Can you get them settled? I have a terrible headache. I need to lie down."

Kory nodded and cleared her throat. She never liked to hear her mother complain of head issues—not since the seizures. Worry rid her mouth of the words she intended to launch, and instead she called, "Smith. Wesson. Inside." With a sweep of her arm and a point to the door, the dogs beat Kory to the porch.

Mom trudged alongside her.

"How was he when you left?" Kory asked as she slid a hand under her elbow and helped her up the steps.

She sighed again. "He looks good, honey. Real good."

The rosy outlook was usually something to admire, but through all of this, it grew more and more unnerving. Did she honestly think he looked good? Or was it denial? As a doctor, denial wasn't something Kory liked to see. Although some people confused it with hope, denial was different; it could be very damaging. She saw it keep patients and their loved ones from their full potential all the time.

But this was her mother and father she was talking about, and it was hard to remain stoic and objective when someone you loved was hurting.

Inside the house, Kory shooed the dogs into the kitchen while Mom settled on the couch. The big silver bowl on the floor was empty, so Kory filled it with water from the tap, and returned it to the center of a ceramic tile square again. All the while she wondered how and when to announce she wasn't returning to Chicago yet. Maybe in the morning, after Mom's headache passed.

Movement behind her caused Kory to turn, and when she did, she saw her mother rummaging through an upper cabinet.

"What do you need?" Kory asked, walking to the cabinet. "Go back and lay down. I'll get it for you."

"I can get it."

"I know you can, but I'm here, so you don't have to."

"I don't want to be dependent. Who do you think's going to take care of me when you're gone?" Her eyes closed and she froze mid-motion—all except her hand, which was trembling as it rested on the cupboard shelf. "I don't want to be a burden. I don't…"

Watching Dad become dependent was taking its toll. Kory pulled her close. "Mom, it's okay. Everything's going to be okay."

As she listened to her mother's muffled sobs, Kory knew the dam of denial had broken and felt some measure of relief. While she would never be so vague as to proclaim things would be "okay" to a patient's family, she couldn't help murmuring that bit of comfort now. Kory badly wanted to believe it herself.

Reaching over her mother's head, Kory retrieved the bottle of pain reliever. "You're exhausted. I see it all the time with patient's families. All this back and forth to the hospital. All this worry keeping you awake. You need to sleep. I can prescribe you something if you want me to."

Mom shook her head against Kory's shoulder. "No. That won't be necessary." Then she lifted her head and wiped the wet from beneath her eyes. "I'll make some chamomile tea. I'll be fine."

Kory inhaled through her mouth and rolled her eyes until she glimpsed the ceiling. There was never going to be a right time to have this conversation, especially not between now and 10:00 A.M. tomorrow. Exhaling slowly, she looked her mother dead in the eyes. "I'm going to make sure everything is fine. I'm staying in Harmony Falls for a while. Will agreed to hire me as the medical director of Harmony Elder Care."

Mom's mouth opened and closed. Her brows knitted in confusion. "You already have a job in your future."

"Yeah, but that job isn't available yet. Even if it was, it wouldn't help Dad unless you moved to Chicago. And trust me, you could never handle public transportation."

"No." Mom stepped back, shaking her head. "You aren't going to give up everything to stay here and take care of us. What about finishing the fellowship?"

"I'm not giving up anything. I'm delaying it. People take leaves of absence all the time. I talked to Dr. Lunderburn, and he understands. He says he'll work with me when I'm ready to come back."

"Your father will be devastated."

"What kind of daughter would I be if I knew I could help him and I didn't?" It wasn't really a rhetorical question. She could've stopped there and given her mother time to think, but instead raw emotion welled in her chest, and she wielded the one question that nagged her the most. "Why don't you want me here, Mom?"

Except for the soft snoring of a dog, there was no sound. Kory held her breath and waited. She couldn't remember ever fighting with her mother before.

Stress had a way of cracking people.

"I want you here," Mom whispered, the sound so fierce she was hoarse.

Kory nodded, but didn't believe the statement was one-hundred-percent true. "You want me here on vacations and holidays. But if I want to stay longer, like now, when I can help, why are you rushing me back?"

"Because you have important work to do." Her voice grew louder. "Do you know how much we sacrificed to give you everything we never had? Do you care?"

"Of course I care!"

"All those—those science camps in b-big cities! They didn't come cheap, Kory Anne!" She was yelling now.

On one hand, it seemed foolish, arguing about science camp, but on the other hand, this was about so much more.

"I didn't ask for those," Kory snapped.

She hadn't asked, but she didn't fight it either. She had wondered how her parents, a roofer and a librarian on disability after too many seizures could afford to send her, but they'd been so happy about her participation, she'd suppressed the urge to ask.

Mom pressed her lips together and widened her eyes. "You had a gift," she hissed. "Normal children play 'hospital' in their bedrooms with their stuffed animals as patients. You turned Dad's workshop into an infirmary for birds and small mammals when you were ten. That's extraordinary, Kory Anne. You asked me if any household chemicals could be used as anesthesia. What were we supposed to do? Ignore that drive in you?"

"No." Kory softened her voice, trying to calm the anger and confusion stirring inside of her. They'd been through a lot this past week. Emotions were high for everyone. "Mom, I appreciate the opportunities you gave me. I do. I'm just questioning why it was so important for me to be gone every summer. Sometimes if felt like you didn't want me around." Kory threw up her hands. "That's how it feels now, too."

With her hands pressed together in prayer formation and her hiss turned to plea, Mom looked ready to drop to her knees and beg Kory to leave. "You are better than this place."

"That's what you've always told me, but you're here. Dad's here."

Mom closed her eyes and shook her head. "You think we want to be here?"

More silence. Kory stared at her mother, trying to make sense of what she was saying. "I thought you liked it here. Your families are here. Where else would you be?"

Mom pressed a hand to her forehead, covering her eyes. "It doesn't matter anymore." She gave an inhale and then an exhale. And then her hand dropped to her side. "You call that doctor in Chicago and tell him you made a mistake, and then you call Will Mitchell and tell him to find another doctor. Your father and I will be fine." She nodded, turned and left the room.

Kory stared dumbfounded at the empty space. She was missing something, a big piece of the puzzle. There was obviously a reason her success mattered more than her presence.

She thought. Hard. Nothing in her childhood filled with overachievement and parental pride stuck out. No stories of her parents falling short of their own goals. Heck, until her father's stroke, his roofing company was thriving. No hint of a deep dark secret came to mind.

It doesn't matter anymore, Mom had said. But what didn't matter? Kory turned, bracing herself on the countertop, her elbows buckling as emotional exhaustion seeped in. How could she not know the reason behind her parents pushing her away? This was Harmony Falls, where secrets didn't stand a chance. Was it possible her parents managed to keep one? And if so, did it even matter in the face of everything that happened since Kory had been home?

She wasn't used to disappointing anyone, let alone her parents. It was a horrible state to be in, and in her sadness she questioned her decision to stay.

• • •

"Then we sell it. With any luck the public offering will force Valley's hand."

Will closed his eyes to his mother's uncompromising words, words he expected to hear. When he opened his eyes, she was scrutinizing him, a calculating gleam in her eye.

"It's a regrettable course of action, William, but difficult choices must be made. This company didn't remain in business for years by prioritizing friendships over financial solvency." Her lips tightened, no doubt stifling a sigh. "If you can't bring yourself to pull the trigger, then I can. I'll have the for sale sign posted today."

"Don't," Will said, watching her eyes widen. "There's another way." She opened her mouth, but he bulldozed right over her. "I'm hiring Kory Flemming to be the full-time medical director. She'll be here at 10 to sign papers, and before you panic about cost, she was making peanuts as a fellow, so she accepted peanuts here. She's cheaper and better than Lance. All she asked is that we re-open to new admissions"—he paused for a quick breath—"including her father. Seems like a win to me."

His mother's nostrils flared.

"What's wrong with maintaining the home if it helps the people in Harmony Falls and it at least breaks even?" he asked.

"Breaking even is not turning a profit. And we are not a charity, William."

"No, but I was under the impression we had a calling greater than padding our bank accounts. These people, our friends, get injured and old, and they need someplace to go."

She scoffed. "They can go to Rileyville. I want it sold."

He wasn't exactly surprised by her rejection, but the lack of compassion shocked him. She was a ruthless business woman, but even she had to see the problematic position they'd be in if they closed the only nursing home and didn't replace it with something equally as valuable.

Come to think of it, maybe there was more to her harsh perspective than the simple sale of real estate, but what more Will didn't know, and he didn't have time to analyze it. He pushed the thought from his mind and went for something he hoped would tip the scale in his favor. "Justin supports me." And Justin could do no wrong.

"Of course he supports you. Alice and Kory are friends."

"He supports me as someone who would like to be mayor of this town. He recognizes the benefit of having a nursing home within the borough boundaries. Mother, if the CFO of this company supports me, why can't you?"

She stared at him until he fidgeted.

He'd been Chief Operating Officer for six years. In that time, he'd butted heads with his mother once or twice a year. It was never a pleasant experience, and it usually ended with him on the losing end. But her heart attack changed things. He'd picked up the slack while she was recuperating, and she'd never reclaimed full power. Maybe he was crazy, but he hoped that slight edge would help him here.

"Two months, William," she said, pointing one bony finger in his direction. "If you haven't at least broken even in two months, then I'll post the 'for sale' sign myself." He bit back a premature smile. "And another thing, no new funds. Not a penny. Do you understand?"

Will nodded. "I understand."

Two months. He only hoped Kory was as good as she claimed to be.

• • •

Two hours later, Will paced in front of his desk, glancing at the clock above the door every few steps. *Ten-oh-two.* Hardly late enough to declare her a no show, but late enough to make him wonder. If she didn't show, he'd be screwed, and the nursing home would be up for sale.

Kory hadn't looked convinced when she made the proposition. With time to dwell on it, she was bound to see it as desperate and dangerous. She'd probably realized the choice job with the flashy title in Chicago wouldn't wait and her replacements were probably already circling the position like sharks in bloody water. Maybe she was on her way back right now to stake her claim.

The desk phone buzzed, and he jumped, reaching out to hit a button. Georgiana's voice echoed in his quiet office. "Dr. Flemming called."

His heart hardened.

"She waited for the doctor to round on her father, so she's running a bit late. Do you want me to reschedule her so you can get out of here by noon?"

Slowly, his heart started beating again. "No, thank you, but you can go. Enjoy your day."

He hit the button on the phone, ending the call, and then picked up the stereo remote, washing the room in the comforting strains of "Je crois entendre encore." Will's head dropped to the back of his chair, and he closed his eyes. Kory was actually going to go through with it. She was going to take the job.

For the first time in days, Will felt like he'd made progress.

An hour later, Kory walked into his office, casually dressed in knee-length khaki shorts and a lightweight denim shirt. Still, she looked ready to take over the world. Her shoulders were back. Her chin was lifted. And determination carved hard lines all over her face.

"Let's get this over with," she said.

Okay, so he hadn't expected her to cover him in kisses of joy—although he may have dreamed of it—but he also didn't expect the hint of animosity in her voice. Was it directed at him? If it was, her hostility was misplaced. He didn't force her into this position. She came to him.

He stood. "We don't have to rush this."

"My father has days before insurance stops covering his hospital stay. Social workers are badgering my mother with nursing home options, none of which include Harmony Elder Care. I need this to be official, so the admissions ban can be lifted, and I can do something productive beside letting the dogs out twice a day." Her gaze flitted around his desk. "What and where do I sign?"

Now was not the time to notice how the light played on her hair as it rested against her blush cheeks. Nor was it the time to admire the perfect symmetry of her glossy lips. So he pretended he hadn't done either, despite the quickening of his pulse.

Will slid a collection of papers forward. "Tabs mark where you should sign."

She looked behind her, stepped sideways, and then sat in an armchair, pulling the documents off his desk and settling them in her lap. "I'll read them first."

His lips hitched. "You should."

She eyed him from beneath her long bangs. "Why? Did you slip something in here?"

"Like what?"

"I don't know. But I don't trust you."

"That's an awful thing to say to your new boss."

"Fuck you," she said, shooting him a snotty grin and then returning her attention to the papers. "There. I'd say that's worse."

Will laughed, because he just didn't know what else to do. She wasn't anything like the awkward girl she used to be. She didn't cower around him, and she didn't even respect him apparently. It was more appealing than it should have been.

His laughter died as he watched her read. Clear, clean fingernails picked at the papers' corners. She used to wear glasses in high school. He wondered if she still did. Maybe at night while she was pouring over medical books. Did she ever slip the curved end of her frames between her lips and suck? Did she bite down, hard?

Damn. Maybe he had a latent librarian fetish, because his skin was heating to clammy proportions.

Under different circumstances—a wedding reception perhaps—he'd pursue her, take a chance. He'd have little choice with the way his body was reacting. But things had changed since his brother's wedding and Will's indiscretions in the coat checkroom. As he watched Kory roll a pen between slim fingers, he reminded himself he was now her boss, and bosses didn't pursue employees.

There were laws against that.

She glanced at him again. "It looks pretty standard."

"It is."

The pen hovered over the first signing point. "I swear to God, Will, if you make me regret this, I'll hurt you."

Twisted as he was, that was a promise he'd like to see her keep.

CHAPTER SEVEN

Kory locked herself in the staff bathroom, gripped the cold porcelain edges of a remarkably outdated sink complete with a rust ring around the drain, and looked her reflection in the eye. "We aren't in Chicago anymore."

Blowing out a big breath, she glanced at the suspended ceiling, yellow with age and water damage. The protein bar she ate for lunch gurgled in her gut, and for the millionth time today she wondered if her father wouldn't be better off in a newer facility in Rileyville. But it was really, truly too late for thoughts like that now. She signed a contract. She'd have to make do, which meant smiling even though most of the staff saw her as the devil incarnate.

Valley Hospital System's decision to back out of the nursing home deal had nothing to do with Kory, but by the way the nurses snickered and stared, they didn't seem to know that. Five minutes into her first day, she'd overheard Margie Croft say, "Everyone knows Kory Flemming only wants to help her father, and then she's out of here. To hell with the job security the rest of us want. Well, to hell with her!" It was hardly a welcome wagon.

And that was before she bumped into Gertrude, who looked at Kory pointedly and asked, "Were you interviewing for the job in the coat checkroom?"

Kory's stomach gurgled again. The naysaying and gossip shouldn't bother her. She was thick-skinned. She'd been called a fucking moron too many times to count by snarly surgeons twice her size. Still, the way these women doubted her *did* bother her.

She looked herself deep in the eyes again and mouthed, "Get a grip. Prove them wrong. It's only temporary."

The knob jiggled, followed by a knock. "Just a minute," she called. When she stepped out Bev was waiting, a smile on her face, but she looked torn when she saw it was Kory. Then she simply nodded and pushed past into the ladies room.

At least she didn't spit on me, Kory thought. She'd been spit on before, but that was during a psych rotation in an architecturally stunning mental health hospital staffed by the nation's top physicians and therapists. Somehow, being spat on in those surroundings was more appealing. What did that say about her? It didn't matter. None of it mattered except getting her father well. The faster she got him well, the faster she could reclaim her life in Chicago.

"Dr. Flemming, Mr. Pell needs his toenails trimmed."

Kory turned around to face a young nurse she didn't recognize, one of the few people in the home who didn't have a history here. "Okay, then let's consult podiatry."

Her face crinkled. "The closest podiatrist is in Rileyville, and he doesn't make trips to Harmony Falls."

Slowly, Kory understood. "I have to trim his nails."

The nurse nodded. "He's diabetic, and it's facility protocol for a doctor to perform the task."

Toenails. Kory held back a grimace. This was something she'd never be asked to do in Chicago where podiatrists and resident podiatrists roamed the halls in numbers equal to nurses. *Rural medicine*, Kory thought. She wasn't sure she was cut out for this. But once again she swallowed her discomfort and performed the task in the name of her father.

When Mr. Pell's toes were hangnail-free, Kory walked the hall at a lightening pace she'd grown accustomed to while following attendings around major hospitals. As she went, she glimpsed empty room after empty room—not just void of patients but equipment, too. The last few days, she'd been acclimating to protocol and the handful of patients under her care. Now, it was time to focus on the facility. She needed furniture in the empty rooms if she wanted to fill this place with patients.

"Excuse me," she called to the jumpsuit-clad body sticking halfway out of the janitor's room.

Cliff Brown poked his head around the floppy head of a mop. "Afternoon, Dr. Flemming. What can I do ya for?"

"Hi, Cliff. Where is the equipment room?"

The skin on his wide nose crinkled. "I'm not sure what you mean."

"Where do you keep the extra furniture? You know, beds, chairs, dressers?"

"Ah. In the junk room. Second door past the boiler room. You'll need a key." He pulled a massive collection of metal attached to a retractable cord from his belt.

Kory watched him fiddle with the keys until he found the one he was looking for. Calling it the junk room didn't leave her feeling warm and fuzzy, but what did she expect? Surely they hadn't stored the good stuff in order to happily use the bad.

"I don't usually give out my keys, but I trust you." He winked. "I remember when you was in diapers." And then he nodded solemnly. "So sorry about your dad. I get to Rileyville a couple times a week for diesel in my truck, and I check on him when I can."

Kory might not readily admit it, but there were some benefits to living in a small town. Cliff, knowing and caring enough about her father to visit him at a hospital thirty miles away was definitely one of those benefits. The fact that Cliff remembered her diaper days?—Not so much. Regardless, she relayed her appreciation with a smile as she accepted the key, and then she thanked God at least one person around here was happy to see her. It was an unexpected boost that put pep in her step as she set out in search of "the junk room."

Her mood plummeted the minute she flipped a switch, illuminating the equipment room with harsh overhead lights that crackled and popped until two went dark, casting shadows that made what was there look even dingier: tables with missing legs and chairs with exposed stuffing. She walked to the nearest bed and pulled on the guardrail. It came off in her hand.

How was she supposed to fill a nursing home that didn't have beds? And why in God's name did they feel the need to lock this room? Who would steal this stuff? Junk room, indeed.

On a huff, she left and headed straight for Fran's office. She found the nursing home director with her head down, typing frantically.

Kory knocked. Fran kept typing.

"Do you have a minute?" Kory asked.

"Not really, but if you don't mind me typing while you're talking, shoot."

"How much money is in the budget for new furniture?"

Fran laughed. Her fingers never skipped a beat. "None. We're lucky we have a line item for bedpans."

"How are we supposed to fill rooms without beds?"

"Welcome to my world."

"Surely we can move some things around. Can't we take some money from the rec therapy department?"

Fran laughed louder. "You've been in Chicago too long, Dr. Flemming. Rec therapy." She shook her head. "Rec therapy at H.E.C consists of Bev reading romance novels to Mrs. Park on Sunday nights."

"Can't we ask the Mitchells for a larger budget?"

Fran's fingers stilled. She rolled her eyes in their sockets until they locked on Kory. "This home is destined for sale. Any money put into the place is wasted money. The Mitchells are already doing everything they can."

Of course. Don't dare challenge the Mitchells. Fortunately for Kory, she'd been challenging one Mitchell most of her life. And the thought of challenging him one more time didn't even make her blink.

•••

Will removed the straw from his Coke and took a hearty drink from the rim, wishing for whiskey. Tuesday lunches with his mother at the Main Street Diner had a way of making him reach for a bottle of aspirin and an alcoholic chaser.

She tapped a boney finger on the table and glanced around the busy restaurant, satisfaction glistening in her eyes. She was a piece of work, no doubt counting up the number of lunch-hour patrons. She was the ever-shrewd businesswoman with a vested, financial interest in the property. Will admired that, even as he hated being made a spectacle. These weekly lunches with her sons were a manipulation. Knowing the town thrived on gossip, the place was packed with people hoping to overhear a juicy tidbit from the Mitchells' table. It was his mother's contribution to uptown business. The rest of the week, lunch receipts might be slow, but Tuesday, by God, would carry those days. The gleam in her eyes told Will she took all the credit.

"Logging truck traffic has increased on Clairburg Road," she said in a stage whisper. "We need to do something about that."

Mark smirked. "Tell him why."

Will drank again, swallowing ice and all. *This ought to be good.*

She glared at Mark. "Why don't *you* since you find it so amusing?" She backhanded his bicep. "There is nothing funny about farm animals refusing to mate."

Will closed his eyes and shook his head. Maybe there wasn't anything funny about environmental stress impacting a farmer's bottom line, but there was definitely something funny about his prim and proper mother talking about farm animals mating.

"We don't own the road, Mother," Will said. "So what would you suggest as a solution?"

"Some Barry White and candlelight might work." Mark chuckled as he bit into his sandwich. He flinched even though Mother didn't raise a hand this time.

"Be serious," she hissed.

"Fine." Mark put down his sandwich and picked up his napkin, wiping it across his mouth. "I say we open up that old logging road that runs through the back half of the golf course. A bunch of ancient golfers can deal with a few weeks of deafening noise better than pigs in heat."

She hit him then.

Will laughed, but he nodded, too, because he agreed with Mark. "Sounds reasonable."

Despite the low hum of conversation and the clang of gathered plates, Will heard the bell above the front door and instinctively looked up as Kory walked in. She stopped in the middle of the restaurant, sliding oversized sunglasses onto her head. Her other hand gripped a cell phone, and she appeared to be scanning the room, looking for someone. He had the oddest wish she was looking for him...until their eyes connected and her mouth twisted.

On second thought, hopefully she was looking for someone else.

But Kory didn't look away, and she *definitely* didn't look happy. Will shot a quick glance at his mother, who was stirring sweetener into her iced tea, and an impulsive flush of protectiveness sent him to his feet. His mother wouldn't find Kory's short-tempered treatment of him as amusing as he did, and if this impromptu visit had anything to do with the nursing home, it could be disastrous in his current company.

"William?" Mother looked up from the swirling liquid.

"Finish without me. There's something I have to take care of." And he was gone from the table, striding across the restaurant, meeting Kory at the midpoint. He smiled, overly bright. "Walk with me."

"Why?" Of course she didn't take his cue. Her brows bunched and her upper lip hitched.

"We have an audience." He didn't need to glance behind him to know his mother was on to him by now.

Fortunately, Kory had lived in Harmony Falls long enough to understand his short explanation, and she turned, silently walking alongside him until they reached the street and relative privacy.

"We need to talk," she said, eyes locked on something farther up Main Street. "I called your office first, and Georgiana told me where you were."

Georgiana's disclosure was odd. Any other time, she micromanaged and guarded his itinerary. The thought raised his brows, but then he relaxed, deciding she was probably hoping to get him out of the barely productive lunch he always complained about.

He tucked his hands in his pants pockets, gathering the edges of his suit coat behind him. "What's up?" he asked, starting aimlessly down the block, mildly concerned by Kory making an appearance.

She kept his pace, matching him stride for stride. The clip-clop of her shoes had him glancing at her feet. Shiny, sensible, round-toed heels peeked from beneath crisply pressed slacks. "We need money to buy new furniture for the home," she said. "Anything usable is taken. What's left is broken. Filling this nursing home is already a longshot, and I can't even try without beds."

Looking up and ahead again, Will veered right, off the main drag, and headed for the elementary school park and the stone bench, bearing his father's name, gracing the butterfly garden on an edge of green. If he was going to be forced to talk about a lack of money, he needed to sit down.

With his hands pushing deeper into his pockets, he filled his lungs with warm summer air. "I'm sure you talked to Fran about this first."

"Of course I talked to Fran. Going over the nursing home director's head to the nursing home owner isn't likely to win me friends, and believe me, I don't need any more enemies."

He stopped walking. She stopped, too. "Who's giving you trouble?" he asked, looking at her, squinting into the sun until the skin around his eyes tightened. He didn't like the idea of anyone but him giving her a hard time. Even in high school when other guys followed his lead it bothered him.

She tipped her head to one side, dragging the sunglasses off her head, catching a glistening wisp of bronze hair between her parted lips. With a hooked finger, she worked against a light breeze to tug the strand free. "That's not important." The wind picked up again and more hair whipped her cheek. Kory laced her fingers through the very top of her hair, raking it back, only to have the same errant strand land between her lips again.

Will wasn't thinking straight, because the next thing he knew his left hand escaped his pocket, and his fingers brushed across her cheek while he picked the strand from her lips and tucked it behind her ear.

Wide-eyed shock registered on her face. She righted her head, closed her lips and swallowed hard, drawing his attention to her neck. God, he was in trouble. Big, fat, lust-driven trouble, the kind that told him to plant his mouth at the base of her throat, right here, right now, consequences be damned.

"I like it better when we fight," she said. The words barely registered beyond the rush of blood in his ears.

"Me, too," he said, staring at the damn intoxicating dip in her throat.

Several heartbeats echoed before anyone moved or spoke again.

"Money, Will. I need more money." The dip undulated with every raspy word.

He managed to drag his attention back to her beautiful face, now mildly distorted with frustration. "There isn't more money until the home starts making money."

Kory furrowed her brow, wrinkling her nose. "I know how it works. I do. I just thought maybe you could make something happen. You're Will Mitchell, you know?"

Yeah. He knew. The name came with a power that wasn't always the picnic people made it out to be. Like now, when he'd like nothing better than to give Kory what she wanted. "I can't make sweeping changes to an individual business's budget without it being put to a vote. I can tell you right now, my mother will not agree. She's already told me no more money is to be appropriated to the home. She wants it sold."

"I understand that, Will, but a thriving home would bring a higher price," Kory said, lifting her chin in challenge.

"In my opinion, a thriving home wouldn't need to be sold."

She bit into her bottom lip and quieted for a moment. "Then why can't we do that? We hold every record of achievement this town has ever known. You have the business mind. I have the medical mind. Can you imagine what we'd be capable of if we banded together?" Her lips pressed shut.

Will could imagine it, because ever since the kiss in the coat closet, he'd been wondering why two people with so much physical chemistry had to be otherwise so far apart.

But maybe they were closer than he'd thought.

"I don't want to see those women out of work, and I don't want to be forced into a desperate deal," he said. "I will support you as much as I can, but finding you more money is a longshot." Which was an understatement considering his mother's warning. There was no way she'd change her mind on that when she was already feeling usurped by Will not agreeing to an immediate sale.

Kory nodded, and then a smile lit her face. "I believe in your capabilities, Will, and you don't know how much it pains high school me to say that. It's just that historically speaking, you don't fail. And once I have beds, I won't fail, either. I'll fill them. I have some ideas. If your mother needs to hear those, I'd be happy to put them into a formal presentation. I can sell her on you, if you can sell her on me."

They stood there staring at each other, that same heightened awareness between them.

"This is weird," he finally said, borrowing from the assessment she'd made while in his driveway. "I do believe you're cheering me on, Ms. Flemming."

"Dr. Flemming," she corrected, and shrugged as she backed away, a crooked smile tilting her lips. "Because this time when you win, I win."

Boy, he liked the sound of that. Impossible though it seemed, he was going to find her that money, because he wouldn't let her down.

CHAPTER EIGHT

Until Will was able to provide the nursing home with a much-needed infusion of cash, Kory was going to have to improvise. Every day the home went unfilled was another day it didn't make money, and at this point, it was the strongest way to determine her success or failure. Pouring over the budget with Fran produced barely enough money to buy one bed. *It's a start*, Kory thought, temporarily shelving the idea to buy new furniture and heading for the junk room to take a second look. Maybe fixing what was already there could yield better results.

An hour later, she had her first open bed…but unfortunately not because of her efforts in the junk room. A code had summoned her to Mr. Martin's room minutes before the man passed away.

He was ninety-eight with a DNR, but the inevitability of the man's death didn't lessen the blow. Mr. Martin had been her piano teacher until the eighth grade. And while he wasn't coherent during her time at the home, every time she lifted his translucent hand to take his pulse, she remembered those fingers flying maniacally across the keyboard. He played sixty-fourth notes like it was nobody's business.

At the end of her shift, Kory had returned to his now-empty room, and sat on the end of the freshly-made bed, staring at the peach-colored cinderblock wall. Her throat burned from swallowing down tears she refused to shed.

It was, for all intents and purposes, her first patient loss. Oh, she'd been there when patients coded. She'd scrubbed in on surgeries that went awry. But she was part of a team then, surrounded by doctors more knowledgeable than her. Here, she was on her own. And here, she *knew* these people.

"You okay?"

Kory turned toward the sympathetic voice and blinked a few times when she saw Bev. Maybe it was an apparition brought on by extreme emotions. Bev wasn't Kory's biggest fan.

Kory nodded, more than a little embarrassed at being caught off her game, but she didn't try to make up an excuse. She didn't know what she could say to explain her behavior anyway.

Bev walked into the room and offered a small smile. "He was a nice man. Nice family, too."

Oh, God. That was supposed to make Kory feel better, wasn't it? She squeezed her eyes shut and swallowed, pushing out thoughts of the nice family, which included a daughter not far from Kory's age, a daughter who was now mourning. The scenario hit a little too close to home. But it wasn't the same as Kory's father's stroke. Mr. Martin's time had simply come, and with a "do not resuscitate" in place, there was nothing anyone could do but make him comfortable.

"His daughter called a few minutes ago," Bev continued. "She wanted to thank you for being there, for holding his hand."

Had she done that? Kory couldn't remember. It was all so hazy. She remembered Bev being there, and the way Mr. Martin's final breaths rattled until Kory could feel them in her bones. Another first. In Chicago, nurses handled the details of dying; doctors simply called the time when a DNR expired. Until now, Kory had never known the hopelessness of watching someone die when she'd sworn an oath to heal.

She nodded, hoping the motion would unclog her throat.

"If you want to talk about it, I'm here. I'll listen."

Now there was a novel idea. Talk about feelings? That was almost scarier than feeling in the first place.

"I'm good," Kory said, standing and smoothing the front of her white coat.

A flash of understanding lit Bev's eyes, and she smiled again. "Okay."

Kory's first few steps felt odd, like she wasn't walking on solid ground. It might take a while for her to feel normal again. After all, she'd just held the hand of a dying man, and then found commiseration in the most unlikely place.

It was funny. She could remember scanning chapters on grief and loss in her university textbooks, a reading assignment that hadn't even warranted any substantial class lecture time. Kory's mouth twisted wryly. Fat lot of good the education she was so proud of had done her this week. Because the way she felt right now?

They didn't teach this stuff in med school.

• • •

The next several days were a blur of getting Kory's father admitted to Harmony Elder Care and then getting him settled. When she wasn't seeing patients, dragging conversation out of her mother or trying to win over skeptical staff, she was working with Cliff to repair the salvageable furniture, because the money she'd hoped for hadn't miraculously appeared.

Each night when Kory crawled exhausted into bed and dropped her head to the pink-cased pillow in her bedroom, satisfaction carried her off to sleep. She might not be preparing to present her research findings at the single biggest gathering of rehabilitation experts from around the world, but she was making a difference. It surprised her how similar the payoff felt.

Now, to get her father up and moving again… She could only imagine the satisfaction in that.

Determined to make this week her most productive week yet, Kory charged into Monday, despite her mother's disapproving glance at the tool box Kory was loading into the bed of the pick-up truck.

"You could be carrying a fancy mocha coffee into a big hospital in Chicago right now."

"I like my coffee and my chocolate separate," Kory said, smiling, fighting hard not to let the chasm between them widen. But it wasn't easy, especially when part of Kory wanted to prod for more answers. A nervous clench of her heart was the only thing keeping her from pushing the issue. Considering her father's condition, they already had enough to deal with.

One family crisis at a time, she reminded herself as she climbed into the pick-up truck and headed to work with her mother in tow.

A mile down the road, Kory couldn't stand the quiet anymore, and since her father's radio hadn't worked since she was in undergrad, she glanced at her mother and spoke. "Do you have any questions about his care?" Maybe it would help to treat her like the family member of any other patient.

Mom shook her head, clutching her purse in her lap, locking her eyes on the rural scene beyond the windshield.

Kory nodded, knowing her best intentions to avoid the topic of their argument in the kitchen wouldn't matter if this kept up much longer.

"Alice and Justin come home soon," Kory said, trying a different approach. "Alice married? That's going to be weird."

Mom nodded again and this time a small smile lit her face. "Talk about weird. She's going to be First Lady of Harmony Falls."

Kory smiled, too. "Well, Justin hasn't won the election yet."

"He will. The Mitchells win everything."

How many times had Kory heard those words? Said those words? Especially where Will was concerned? This time, she didn't bristle. She only hoped to God when it came to money for the nursing home he would be victorious again.

The rest of the drive was painfully quiet.

Once Kory parked in her official spot under the sign labeled "Medical Director," she retrieved the toolbox from the back of the truck. She would round on patients first, and then get to work on furniture repair.

Mom didn't wait. She walked ahead, disappearing inside the home.

The cold shoulder routine twisted Kory's lips, but she refused to let her mother's puzzling behavior negatively impact the day.

"Morning, Jane," Kory called to the woman behind the reception desk.

"Morning." Jane's normally indifferent greeting was punctuated by an almost-sneer as her eyes shifted in the direction of the main hall.

Apparently, there was something in the hall Jane wanted Kory to see. With a breath into her mouth, Kory made the turn, coming face to face with giant boxes and a sweaty, red-faced Fran.

"What's this?" Kory asked, placing a hand on the nearest box.

"You asked for beds, didn't you?"

"Thank you, God," Kory said, glancing at the ceiling.

Fran rolled her eyes. "Don't you mean, 'Thank you, Will Mitchell?' I told you not to bother him," she added, leaning closer and lowering her voice.

"I didn't *bother* him. I just..." But Fran walked away.

Kory followed. "I asked for more money for beds. What's wrong with that?"

"That's not the way to run a business. Budgets are set and followed for a reason."

"Of course, but I don't see how this is a bad thing. If Will added more money to the budget..."

Fran stopped and faced Kory. "He didn't *add* more money to the budget. Business doesn't work like that. And the invoice says, 'Sold to Will Mitchell.' He must have purchased the beds with his own money."

"No." Hospital beds were easily a thousand dollars each. Kory counted twenty boxes. That was an awful lot of personal money to invest in this place when it was underperforming. "Why would he..." The words caught in her throat on memories of their conversation.

I believe in your capabilities. She'd told him that. Had he taken the challenge too far?

Fran shot a glance at Gertrude who was eavesdropping from the corner. "Well, since you're asking me, I'd say it's because you either badgered and guilted him into it or he did it as a personal favor." She hit the word *favor* hard with a twist to her lips. "You know, if Valley comes back around, looking to buy again, which is what Margaret Mitchell is hoping for, and this is a full, thriving nursing home, all you'll have done is driven up the price of this place and ensured almost fifty people will be displaced. But who cares, right? You'll be long gone by then. You got your beds. You proved you could fill them. You win."

When it was put that way, it didn't sound like winning.

The beds and Fran's assertion Kory "guilted" Will into spending personal money he might not be able to recoup bothered her all day. He'd gone out on a limb for her at her request, and it felt like an incredibly intimate thing to do. The pressure to succeed so his investment didn't fail was alarming. But what exactly constituted as success? Fran's perspective seemed aligned with Mrs. Mitchell's and contrary to Will's. Which one was right?

If Kory really wanted to know, then she was going to have to ask Will.

After dinner, Kory stayed home with the dogs while her mother and Aunt Jeanie took the evening shift with her father. She settled into an Adirondack chair on the patio and nursed an oversized glass of red wine, thinking of Will. Again. She thought about calling him to get to the bottom of this, to ask point blank if he invested personal money in the nursing home, and why he thought it was a good idea. Then she needed to know what she had to do to make his investment viable. Again, it felt too intimate, like a line of propriety had been crossed. *A personal favor*, Fran had said. Was it because of the kiss?

Neither one of them had breathed a word of it since. With her phone in one hand and wine in the other, Kory went so far as to bring up his contact information. She drank as the dogs barked in the distance and she stared at the name and number, trying to decide exactly what she should do.

Eventually, exhaustion from the busy day fueled by wine set in, and she closed her eyes instead.

• • •

Will blinked at the lighted screen. He couldn't say the caller's name surprised him—he figured Kory would have something to say about the beds—but he was disappointed she resorted to calling instead of paying him another unannounced visit. He wanted to see her again.

"Hello," he said.

Dogs barked in the distance and shuffling sounded on the other end, but no words returned his greeting.

"Kory? Hello?"

Nothing but more muffled sounds. *Butt dial*, he thought, hanging up, oddly satisfied by the idea of her butt picking him. But then another less satisfying thought hit him. What if it wasn't a butt dial? What if something was wrong? He'd left the nursing home ten minutes ago, and her mother had been there. If something was wrong, Kory was facing it alone.

Will called her back.

When she didn't answer, he decided a perfect gentleman would stop by her house and make sure she was okay. Never mind her house was five miles away and in the opposite direction from his.

Never mind the inner voice accused him of using this as an excuse to see her again.

By the time his Mercedes was dodging potholes on the dirt road leading to Kory's house, he had himself thoroughly convinced this was the rational, chivalrous thing to do.

Lights on. That's a good sign, he thought as he pulled down the long drive.

For some reason, he shrugged out of his jacket and draped it across the passenger seat before stretching out of the car. Humid night air stuck to his skin as he walked the pavers to the porch. He loosened his tie.

Perfect gentleman, he reminded as his knuckles met a pane of frosted glass on the wood front door.

The dog's barked, the sound getting closer, but still muffled by the door, and then a long, lean shadow flickered on the other side of glass.

Kory opened the door slowly, revealing just her hand around one dog's neck first, and then her emerald eyes peaked around the edge. They widened as her brows lifted, and she pulled the door back. "Smith and Wesson, lay down."

Will glanced at the dogs trotting from her side, and then gave her a full-body appraisal. "I see you're okay," he said, desperately trying to stick to the chivalry plan. It wasn't easy. Tiny straps of a pale yellow, breast-hugging tank top bit into the curves of her shoulders, and a flimsy pair of plaid boxer shorts revealed miles of buttery leg. The vision sapped the chivalry right out of him.

"Of course I'm okay. Why wouldn't I be?"

At the sound of her voice, he dragged his attention away from her body and back to her face. "You called me, but when I answered no one was there. I called back, but you didn't answer. I didn't know what to think."

"So you drove all the way over here?"

"Yes."

She rolled her green-eyed gaze to the porch ceiling and exhaled through pouty lips. "My call was a mistake. I didn't answer when you called back, because I wasn't ready to talk to you."

She was always the straight shooter. He nodded. What could he say to that? Silence was the best option if he wanted to remain the perfect gentleman.

"But, since you're here," she continued. "We should talk about the beds."

There was an "s" on the end of the word. He knew exactly which beds she was talking about, and yet the orb of immaturity masquerading as his brain wanted to talk about one bed in particular—the bed they could share.

"What about the beds?" he managed, stressing the "s."

She squinted, looking at him funny for a minute. "Did you buy them with your own money?"

"Yes, I did. You needed beds, didn't you?"

"I did, but I figured the purchase would be made through the business somehow. Fran says either I guilted you into it or you did it as a *personal* favor."

"You didn't guilt me into anything."

"So it was a *personal* favor?"

Sort of, but he needed her to succeed, too, and his mother wasn't going to approve of company money to help either of them.

Will exhaled, and for the first time in his life where Kory Flemming was concerned, he put it all out there in the simplest terms. "Yes, it was a personal favor. My mother refused additional company money for the nursing home. What was I supposed to do? You needed beds, so I bought them for you, and I believe with them you will succeed."

Her face softened, her lips parted, and a blast of heat nearly knocked him off his feet. He reached for words to anchor him in the spot where he stood, because he was seconds away from wrapping her up in his arms and pushing inside in search of a bed of the non-hospital variety.

"That's an expensive vote of confidence," she said, her brows slipping beneath her bangs.

"You're more than worth it." He stepped forward, just a half inch, really, but damn it if he didn't know he was about to screw things up. It didn't matter. He stepped forward again.

Kory shook her head. "This is a bad idea, Will."

"I've had a lot of them lately."

"Me, too," she said, exhaling, reaching out to graze his red tie with her bare fingertips.

It was so hesitant, so innocent, that it broke him. He grabbed her wrist as she grabbed his tie, and they collided just inside the open door. Their lips pressed together, and he watched from the awkward angle as her eyelids fluttered and closed.

This really was crazy, wasn't it? Better take advantage of the lack of sanity while it lasted.

He opened his mouth and welcomed her in as he reached behind him with his foot, hooking it around the edge of the door and kicking it shut.

"My mom will be home at nine. Like clockwork." Her lips slipped and nipped at his, while her heavy, wine-scented breath warmed him.

When was the last time he had to worry about a parent walking in on him? Something about that turned him on full blast, and every inch of him went hot and hard. He let go of her wrist and slid his hand around her waist to the small of her back where he dipped fingers beneath the elastic of her shorts. With his other hand, he reached up and yanked open his tie.

She had him shirtless in seconds, clawing his pecs and then her hands were on his shoulders, pulling him along as she walked them backward.

To the couch, he thought when he opened his eyes for a quick look. But then her hands were on his face, and her tongue was deep inside his mouth and the consummate planner in him didn't care where they were headed, as long as it ended up with them both naked.

He gripped the hem of her tank top and lifted it over her breasts, sliding his palms over the hardened points, letting the weight of her fill his hands. Blood rocketed through his veins, leaving a blazing trail in its wake.

She finished the job of removing her shirt, lifting it over her head and tossing it to the floor. "This can't mean anything, Will. We already have enough to worry about without adding relationship overtones to the mix. It's just sex."

Fine with him, but he couldn't help adding a, "What if I'm really good?" He rolled her nipples between his thumbs and forefingers, reveling at the heavy-lidded look on her face.

She shuddered. "Then it was a really good nothing. Now shut up before I change my mind." She dropped to the couch, pulling him along for the ride.

This was one time he wouldn't argue. He'd keep his mouth damn good and busy to make sure of that.

CHAPTER NINE

It had been a while. That's how she rationalized her current position—flat on her back with Will Mitchell, the man who was now signing her paychecks, sucking her breast. She knew enough about human sexuality to know gaps in intimacy could lead some people to desperation. And she'd had gaps. Big gaps. Because sex wasn't a high priority on her achievement list.

He flicked his tongue across her nipple while his fingers dipped between her legs.

Kory moaned. *Yep, desperate.* But at this point, why fight it? She was long overdue for an orgasm by someone else's hand.

Letting go of thought, she drifted in a fog of pleasure, bombarded by sensation until she gripped him by his soft black hair to keep from floating away.

Orgasm pulled a guttural noise from her throat, and she lay tingling beneath him while he tugged her shorts from her hips.

"How much do you want to bet I can make you come again?" he asked in between kisses to her belly.

Kory's eyes snapped open, and she lifted her head off the cushion to look at him. "You are not going to make this a competition are you?"

He smiled, dragging his mouth lower. "What if I did?"

She laughed, but when his mouth hit the still-warm spot between her legs, there wasn't anything funny about it. She'd never had back-to-back orgasms. She wasn't sure she was capable of it. Nobody else had ever tried. Biting into her bottom lip and writhing beneath the pressure from his tongue, she figured it was just like Will Mitchell to be the overachiever.

"What kind of bet is this?" Her voice raised an octave when his finger slipped inside of her. "Am I really supposed to bet against you?"

He glanced up at her, eyes dark. "Seems foolish," he said with a wicked grin.

It did. She returned her head to the pillow, running a hand through his hair in surrender. This was one time she wasn't going to mind losing.

The second orgasm took longer than the first, but that only made it stronger.

Will crawled over her, planting kisses on the path until he reached her mouth and plundered her. When he finally pulled back enough that she could look him in the eye, he was smiling. "I win."

Kory smiled back. "Believe me. I'm more than happy to concede."

He kissed her neck and stroked her inner thighs, skirting the throbbing center. "I wonder…"

Kory shook her head. "No. There is no way it will happen again."

He looked at her, brows bobbing. "I love it when somebody tells me 'no way.' It's the ultimate challenge."

"Will," she shook her head again as she worked to free him from his pants. "We're running out of time. Nine o'clock sharp. Remember?"

A groan caught in his throat when she reached down and took him in hand.

"I'd like things between us to be reasonably fair." She grinned as she stroked. "I mean, you can say you won all you want, but as it stands the score is 2-0 me." She hit the "oh" a little hard and breathy. "Seems like you're losing."

He captured her mouth with his.

Seconds later, he was inside her, rocking them gently as he sucked a path from her ear to her breast. She wrapped her legs around him, urging him deeper, feeling her control slipping. Incredulously, she contracted again. *Residual spasm from the last orgasm*, she thought. There was no way she'd had three orgasms in such close succession. It was biologically impossible. Wasn't it?

Will lifted his head and looked at her, long and hard while his thrusts became more frantic.

She expected some sort of braggadocios commentary, waited for it, but the words never came, just a flash of something that momentarily, irrationally frightened her, and then his mouth was on hers again.

This is nothing, she reminded herself.

But suddenly she wasn't so sure.

• • •

Will blocked a gush of ridiculous words by kissing her. He concentrated on the tangle of tongues and the wetness between her legs. The ache in his groin. The hammering in his chest. But the words circled his mind. It wasn't *nothing* like she'd proclaimed it— maybe for her, but not for him. For him it was something, something he couldn't name, but something more than impromptu sex on her parent's couch followed by indifference the next day.

Whatever this was or wasn't, it wouldn't be the end of them.

Those were the words fresh in his head as he drove inside of her. Eventually, there were no more thoughts. Just the sounds of two people pushing each other to the edge. Closer and closer. With each thrust of their hips. And then he was there. Coming undone. Breathing heavy against her ear. She engulfed him with the sweet smell of her hair and the warm cushion of her body. She shuddered beneath, offering a happy sigh.

"That was the best damn *nothing* I've ever had," he whispered.

"Same here." She raked gentle fingertips over his back.

"I guess 2-1 isn't a terrible score."

"3-1," she corrected. "It was faint, but it was there."

He lifted his face from her neck. "Damn, I'm good."

"Maybe I'm just sensitive to orgasm."

"Maybe you're just sensitive to me."

She smiled. "I don't know about that, but what I do know is you're two orgasms behind."

He laughed. "Then I better catch up." Thank God, they'd finally found a healthy release for all the competitiveness.

"Not tonight, Romeo. My mom. Seriously."

Will kissed the dip at the base of her neck. "You're going to have to see me again, Dr. Flemming…so we can even things up a bit. After all, you said you wanted things fair."

"This is crazy, Will. I've already been accused of using *personal favors* to land a job and more beds for the facility, beds that will not make your mother happy. What would people think if they knew about this?"

She was right. Being publicly, personally involved with Kory certainly wouldn't earn him praise from his mother, and it could mean more aggravation for Kory from the nursing home staff. But what good was power if you couldn't wield it once and awhile?

He pushed off of her. "As long as I'm still signing paychecks and making reasonably smart business decisions, I don't care what people think."

He certainly wasn't going to let that stop him from seeing her.

• • •

Kory pushed a wheelchair behind her father who was walking slowly, painfully with help from Ben, his physical therapist, and a hemi-walker. "You're doing great, Dad," she said, because after almost two weeks in the nursing home it was progress to see him up and around. But thank God he couldn't see her furrowing brow.

He was going to need to exhibit more improvement than this if he was ever going to get back home.

"Haa...d," he growled, like a drunk in a Boston bar.

"Yes, it is hard, Mr. Flemming, but hard is good," Ben said, coaxing a few more feet out of the panting, grumbling man before he teetered back into the wheelchair.

Kory patted her father's shoulder and glanced behind her. He'd walked about twenty-five feet. "Good job. Rest a minute and we'll do it again."

Despite his grunted disapproval, he managed another twenty-five feet, along with various leg exercises. Kory felt marginally hopeful about his recovery for the first time since the stroke. When he was resting comfortably in his room with his wife by his side, Kory pulled the physical therapist into the hall.

"Can you stay later today and give him another session?"

Ben raised his brows, but nodded. "Sure, but I can't imagine he'll be happy to see me coming back for more after all that."

"I don't care if he's happy or not at the moment. I care if he's progressing. We both know most of his recovery is going to happen in the first four weeks after the stroke. Look at him. He has a long way to go."

Ben nodded. "I'll do what I can."

The guy was already doing enough, letting her horn in on therapy sessions she never would have thought to attend or been welcomed at in Chicago. She didn't need to be there, but here in this more intimate, personal setting, she felt far more invested in the outcomes. A home with a reputation for successful rehabilitation that resulted in discharges was a home that would shoot to the top of social workers' and families' must-admit lists. She told herself she was doing it for Will, so he could recoup his investment, but she was doing it for herself, too. She liked this hands-on medicine.

Kory thanked Ben and headed off on another informal round of patients. Then, she turned her attention to filling the new beds. Sucking antibacterial-scented air into her lungs, she walked to her office, contemplating what she would say to the social worker at Valley Hospital. "We're open for business," sounded too much like something a restaurant owner might say. She rounded the corner and stepped into the room, coming face-to-face with Will.

He was dressed in the usual—suit and tie. Something similar to what he wore the last time she saw him at her house. When they'd ended up on the couch. Naked.

She gave her head a good shake. This was her workplace, not her bedroom. "Hi. What are you doing here?"

He stepped aside and pointed to her desk. "I brought coffee."

Kory stared at the paper cups; two of them perched alongside a stack of charts. Two. As in a pair. Again, what was supposed to be *nothing* felt like something.

"Thank you, but I didn't ask for coffee," she said.

He grinned. "That's what makes it such a nice gesture."

That's what made it such a dangerous gesture. Will stopping by to have coffee with her brought their personal relationship into the workplace, something she wanted to avoid for both of their sakes. She thought she'd made that clear unless he was here in an official capacity.

"Did we have a meeting that I forgot about?" she asked, staring at the cups, trying not to get swept up in him being two feet away. It was bad enough she could smell his aftershave. Even worse, the spicy scent was making her mouth water.

Will grabbed the nearest cup and raised it to his mouth, touching the tip of his tongue to the steaming spout.

"Nope. I wanted to see you," he said.

Damn. Her heart skipped a beat. This was not good. This was not *nothing*. This felt like a stupid schoolgirl crush. Only, there wasn't anything schoolgirl-appropriate about what happened between them on the couch. And there wasn't anything grown-woman-appropriate about her desire to repeat it right here, right now.

She scrambled around the desk and sat before her knees gave out. "Well, you saw me, and I'm working," she said, adding a laugh to sooth the brushoff. "Thanks for the coffee."

He didn't leave. He sat in a chair beside her. Blasting her with a cloud of sexy, man-scented air. "How's your day going?"

Kory glanced up in time to see him put the cup to his lips. He sipped, sucked really. It reminded her of *other things*. She propped her elbow on the desk, putting an arm between them, and dropped her forehead to her hand. "Good, but I'm really busy, Will. I was about to call Valley about new admissions."

"Don't let me stop you."

When he didn't stand and leave, she looked at him again. "You're going to watch me make a phone call?"

He nodded. "I'd like to watch you do a lot of things."

Her face burned, and the heat from her cheeks blazed a trail down her throat, over her chest until it pooled between her legs. "Have dinner with me." He leaned forward, setting the coffee cup on the edge of her desk. "Tonight at my place."

She swallowed a fresh surge of heat. "I eat with my mom. I don't like her eating alone."

He nodded. "Fair enough. Then have dessert with me?"

He exhaled, and she inhaled, tasting him on her tongue. "What time?"

"Seven o'clock."

She nodded, because by now the heat had sucked every last drop of moisture from her mouth, and words were futile.

Will stood, buttoned his suit coat and smoothed a hand down his striped tie. "I'll see you then," he said with a grin. "Oh, and don't let your coffee get cold."

With the temperature in the room, that was impossible.

• • •

Will left Kory's office wearing a lip-stretching smile, and nearly plowed Fran off her feet. He grabbed her shoulder to steady her. "I'm sorry. I didn't know you were there."

Which begged the questions how long had she been there, and how much had she heard?

"Do you have a minute?" Fran tossed her head to the left, toward her open office door.

"Of course," he said nodding, despite wanting to walk in the opposite direction. Anytime Fran wanted to talk in private, chances were he wasn't going to like her words.

But still, the smile lingered at the corner of his lips. He wondered if Kory liked chocolate cake. Who didn't like chocolate cake?

Fran closed her office door behind him. "Ben came to me for permission to charge overtime."

Will scratched his forehead with the length of his index finger. "Well, I suppose he'll need to be brought back up to full time once all the beds are filled."

"Now. He wants overtime pay *now* to work with Ken Flemming. It seems Dr. Flemming is requesting additional sessions." Fran's lip hitched when she mentioned Kory. "You know she's using us to get her father better."

"Of course she's using us," Will snapped. "We're using her, too." Right? He tried to think of his original, selfish reason for hiring her. It was tied to Valley postponing the deal. It was tied to people like Fran and Ben needing jobs. It was tied to…

"Where are we going to get the money for increased payroll?" She raised her too-skinny, penciled-on brows. "Please tell me it won't come from the same place the bed money came from. Your mother would…"

"Fran," Will held up his hands, trying to halt her downward spiral into melodrama, "it's under control. You don't need to worry about this."

She exhaled loudly, sounding unconvinced. "The more you personally put into this place the more you have to lose when Dr. Wonderful leaves town."

Will didn't want to think about losing anything, not after the conversation he had minutes ago with Kory. She accepted his dessert invitation without a struggle. After that, he was feeling too good about himself to let anyone infer he didn't have what it took to keep "Dr. Wonderful" around—at least longer than she needed to be. Okay. Maybe he was kidding himself she would stay beyond the initial terms of her contract. Then again, maybe she was kidding herself she would leave.

It sounded like one hell of a faceoff to Will.

"Thanks for your concern, Fran. But I really do have it all under control. Trust me," he said, letting the smile he felt on the inside blast across his face. "We'll talk again soon."

Right now, he was on a mission: Locate Harmony Fall's best chocolate cake.

CHAPTER TEN

Kory watched her mother stab garbanzo beans with a fork. One by one she extracted them from her spinach salad, placing them gently between her grim lips.

"Considering the magnitude of his stroke, he's doing well," Kory said, halting her own fork inches from her mouth.

Mom sipped iced tea, sighed and plucked another bean from her salad. "It's hard to see him like that. Day after day after day."

"I know it is. It's hard for me, too." Kory shrugged while she chewed. "But he really, truly is progressing." She still hated that he couldn't walk on his own, but she didn't feel that constant heaviness in her chest anymore. "I wouldn't be here if I didn't believe he could be even better."

It was the wrong thing to say. Kory knew it the minute her mother's eyes widened.

"Well, you know what? It's hard seeing you like this, too. Day after day after day."

"Like what?" This was getting old, especially in light of all Kory was accomplishing. Every night she felt more and more satisfied. Every day she felt more and more hopeful. "I'm doing a lot over there." Today she even managed to throw together a recreational therapy schedule that wouldn't cost Will Mitchell a dime. "I don't see how it's difficult to watch me making a difference in people's lives."

"You know what I mean." More sips of iced tea. More stabbing of beans.

Yeah, Kory knew. Again with the reminder that Harmony Falls wasn't good enough, that Chicago was the goal. All the reminders ever really did was leave Kory questioning how and why she'd become an unwanted guest in her own home.

She set her fork on her plate and pushed back in her chair, not to leave, but to give her indigestion room to breathe. "I wish you'd tell me what this is really about."

The same blank stare that always greeted her when she pried greeted her now.

Frustration made Kory fidget. She wanted the truth, but she couldn't find words strong enough to extract it. "Fine," she conceded. "I'll tell you what. You let me get Dad better, and I'll leave." She snapped her fingers. "Just like that. Then you two can take off for wherever you wanted to be in the first place without me interfering."

Mom sighed as she looked away, and then she gathered her plate. "I'm…never mind. Aunt Jeanie will be here soon."

Kory watched her mother walk away from the table and disappear into the kitchen, a thick sadness filled the air. At least she had Will. Six months ago, if someone would have told her she'd be anxious to spend time with him, she'd have had them committed.

"I'm taking the truck tonight," she called after her mother. "I'll be home late. Don't wait up."

Just like Kory thought, there wasn't another word.

Upstairs, while her mother waited for Aunt Jeanie, Kory showered away the self-pity, annoyed by it in the face of everything she'd managed to accomplish in such a short time. She shampooed twice, conditioned extra-long and shaved every possible inch until the razor slipped effortlessly over her skin. Still, random thoughts about her mother's dissatisfaction arose until Kory was answering them with: *at least somebody wants me*. Okay, so the fact that the somebody was Will Mitchell was complicated, but still… She wasn't wholly unwanted. On the contrary, Will seemed to want her very much.

Right now, Kory needed that.

An hour later, dressed in cutoff button-flies threadbare from too much wear in high school and a red ribbed tank top, Kory slipped her feet into flip flops, snagged a bottle of sweet white wine from her mother's stash and hopped into the truck. Anticipation combined with humidity made it hard to breathe. *Dessert.* It had to be a euphemism for sex. It better be. Hell, she'd taken thirty minutes to pick out her bra and underwear. That was twice as long as it took her to do her hair. But he did ask her to dinner first and dinner was legit. Like a date. Dating Will seemed much crazier than sleeping with him. And not just because it was Will Mitchell, but because Kory didn't date.

Dating was sticky and distracting. It required time and energy Kory didn't have to give, not if she wanted to be taken seriously in an uber-competitive, male-dominated field. She had a couple friends-with-benefits over the years, and that suited her just fine. Now she could add Will.

This isn't a date.

She focused on a wide array of "desserts" the rest of the drive there.

Before she even had a chance to knock or ring the bell, Will opened the door clad in khaki shorts and a polo shirt. He'd been waiting for her. The warm, fuzzy feeling of being wanted expanded her chest.

"Hi," she said, stepping into the glow of the porch light, holding up the bottle of wine. "My contribution to dessert."

He waggled his brows. "Step inside my lair, and I'll show you my contribution."

Yep. *Sex.* She was right. Screw dessert.

Grinning, she followed him into the house, where soft opera met her on the other side of the door. Similar music had played in his office the day of their confrontation. She was about to ask him about his penchant for emotional, complex music when she stepped into the living room. The coffee table was outfitted with wine glasses, china, and the biggest chocolate cake she'd ever seen, perched on a silver pedestal. Classy. Much classier than necessary for what she had in mind.

"Oh." The bottle of wine hung limp at her side. "There really is dessert."

"You look disappointed."

She stared at the impeccably set table. Maybe he didn't want her as much as she thought he did. "I'm not disappointed. I just… Never mind."

He chuckled and reached for her, sliding a hand around her waist, pulling her closer. "We can eat before or after whatever it is *you* had in mind. Chances are I have the same thing in mind, too."

Relief relaxed her, and she wrapped her arms around his neck, dangling the bottle behind him. "Good." She wiggled against his chest. "I was starting to get a complex."

"About what?" He nipped at her lips.

"Being wanted." She nipped back.

He chuckled. "I can fix that."

His hot mouth covered hers, filling her with the woodsy scent of cologne and the fresh taste of mouthwash. His arms locked around her waist, fusing their bodies together, so tight she could barely breathe. And she thanked every higher power in the history of humankind, because this was what she came for: Mind-numbing sex.

Was it too much to hope the numbing could be permanent?

"Come on," he said, his wet lips brushing back and forth across hers. "Follow me."

He grabbed her by the hand and led her out the other side of the living room to a dark hallway. Her heart thrashed. Her mouth burned. But her mind remained pleasantly blank as she watched his powerful strides. Somehow, she had the presence of mind to set the wine bottle on a table as they passed, before he tugged her inside the first room on the right and closed the door.

She blinked against the darkness. As odd as it was to be standing in Will's bedroom, she wasn't going to change her mind about being here. If she weren't here, she'd be home alone...or at the nursing home, where Fran gave her the stink eye, her father was half the man he used to be, and her mother treated her with painful disregard.

"I'm not going to run," she said, smoothing her hand along his forearm. "You didn't have to close the door."

"I know. That's to keep the dog out, and to do this..." He charged her, wrapped her in an embrace, and spun her around until her back hit the door.

"Dramatic," she breathed.

"Drama has nothing to do with it," he said, lips dragging up and down the side of her neck. "It's about leverage." He shoved hands behind her until he gripped her bottom and lifted.

Straddling him, Kory expected a joke about her lack of physics prowess. Nothing but slow, wet kisses came from Will's mouth.

This was new. This was nice. Kory dropped her head against the wooden door amid a rush of lusty anticipation. She'd never been ravished against a door. She opened her eyes as Will continued the thrilling assault on her throat, lowering his mouth to the scoop of her tank top where he could kiss and lick the tops of her breasts. With his body hard against hers, he held her in place, ratcheting her desire.

"*I* want you," he whispered. "Whenever. Wherever." He lifted his head until they were nose to nose and he was staring into her eyes. "You call me anytime you need to be convinced."

• • •

By the time Will was finished with Kory, he'd thoroughly convinced her twice.

"More please," she whimpered.

He laughed against the smooth skin of her belly, planting kisses as he continued upward until he found her mouth. This was beyond perfect, if there were such a thing. Waiting so long to take things this far was a crying shame, because now their time was finite.

Rolling to his side, Will cradled her to his chest, breathing her in, pushing out thoughts of real life. The longer he lay there, the more he was overcome by the oddest sense of right. Kory belonged here. He couldn't pretend it was forever, but right now? Definitely.

Molly whined from the other side of the bedroom door.

"Hold that thought," Will said, not exactly sure which one of them he was talking to.

He pushed off the bed and into his boxers, glancing back as he crossed the room. She sprawled naked and smiling across his bed. Talk about winning.

Opening the bedroom door, his chest puffed with satisfaction, and he patted Molly's head, leading her outside. Hot and sticky air surrounded him as he settled on the top step to watch the dog waddle around her usual patch of yard. Only the dissonance of crickets kept him company as she slipped in and out of the shadows. His mind wandered back to Kory. She was in his bed. The urge to hurry Molly was strong, but it died on his lips as a thought chilled him. She'd been here before Kory, and if he were being honest instead of overly optimistic, he could admit Molly would be here after her, too.

For the first time in a long time he preferred to be overly, blindingly optimistic. He meant what he'd said in that bedroom. He wanted Kory. Whenever. Wherever. But what did that really mean? It would be a lot harder to keep a promise like that once she returned to Chicago.

"Hey."

He turned his head to see her on the other side of the screen door. She was out of his bed sooner than he wanted her to be. Disappointment added to his bewildering introspection.

"Sorry," he said, facing Molly and her geriatric pace. "She takes longer than most dogs."

The screen door creaked behind him, and the cold metal barely touched his back.

"That's okay."

He looked up to find Kory fully dressed. *Great.* Not only was she out of his bed, but she was leaving. He looked away again. Of course she was leaving. She got what she came for.

Will Mitchell was Kory Flemming's booty call. If it weren't so pathetic, he'd be laughing.

Fran's gloomy prediction from earlier in the day made an unwelcomed appearance in his already crowded mind, and he reminded himself he was getting what he wanted, too. So what if Kory was using him in and out of bed? After the way he'd treated her in high school, it was the least he could do. Besides, it was by no means torturous penance.

Rolling back his shoulders and holding his head high, Will braced for her goodbye. He'd take another shot at her tomorrow.

"You want some cake?" she asked instead, her warm hand splaying between his shoulder blades.

It was probably pathetic to feel relief, but he felt it just the same. It spread from the spot beneath her hand through the rest of his body until it loosened his arm enough for him to reach up and wrap around her wrist, not wanting her to leave even if it was only for cake.

"In a minute," he said. "Sit. Talk to me."

She skimmed past him, until she was standing on the patio, and he had no choice but to let go. "About what?"

He inhaled and exhaled, searching for something to keep her there. By his side. Where he swore he didn't need anyone. It was the strangest internal war he'd ever waged. He just never realized how lonely he was until tonight.

"How's work?" he asked.

Her bold brow rose. "Fine."

"How's everyone treating you?"

She wrapped arms across her chest. "There are factions of dissenters, but it doesn't matter. I told you that. I'm there to do a job, not make friends."

He nodded, admiring her focus and sensibility, but wishing everyone would cut her some slack whether she needed them to or not. The happier she was, the easier her job would be. The easier her job was, the more likely she was to linger.

He knew wishful thinking when he saw it, so he attempted to keep things professional, as professional as one could keep things while clad in boxer shorts, post-sex. "So what's your next step... job-wise?" he asked.

Her face had a way of crunching and letting him know she was on to him. "Are you asking as the man I just slept with or as my boss?"

Her gutsy sass made him grin. "Both." They both had different reasons for asking. The man she slept with was more interested in *how* she answered. Was she content enough to hang around? On the other hand, her boss was interested in whether or not her next step would be profitable.

Molly wandered onto the patio, slow and steady, and Kory reached out, placing a hand on the dog's head. "I'm going over to Valley Hospital tomorrow to talk to doctors and patients, hoping to drum up some business. Being hands-on seems to suit me. Who knew?" She nodded, and her eyes widened until they sparkled in the patio lights. If he wasn't mistaken, her lips hinted at a smile.

She had contentment over the job? *Check.* Petting Molly wasn't hurting her mood either and the dog had the same calming effect on him.

"So you're adding liaison to your job description?" He dropped down a couple steps so he could reach Molly, too. She lifted her head so Will could scratch beneath her chin.

"Why not? My dad's progressing. The home isn't full yet, so I have time on my hands. I plan to be aggressive when it comes to new admissions." She petted Molly in long strokes from head to tail.

He liked her drive, but if he were keeping track of all the things he liked about Kory, her ease with animals would be even higher on the list. Accidentally-on-purpose he slid his hand along the side of Molly's head, hooking his index finger around Kory's pinky.

"You're an amazing woman, and I'm so happy you're here."

Kory opened her mouth, and then closed it.

The thoughts were probably better kept to himself. She looked shocked, maybe even scared. The grim line of her lips repeated a familiar facial expression from high school. She wasn't used to sincere compliments from him, so he tried to blame her reaction on the lack of experience. But then she shook her head, and a sense of doom squeezed his chest.

"Will, this is not...we're not...together. I'm not staying." The last three words were delivered matter-of-fact as she lifted her hand away from his and crossed her arms over her breasts again. "This is just some no-strings-attached fun."

It felt like more than that. But she was so damn sure she knew better than him.

The age-old desire to best her kicked in. "I bet I can convince you to stay," Will spouted without thinking.

There was more head shaking. "Don't make this into another competition."

"Why not? We thrive on that, don't we?"

"Chicago is different. There are things there I can't get here. I promise you, it's one time you won't win."

Will grunted and stared beyond her into dark space. Him? Not win? Never.

"Challenge accepted, Dr. Flemming," he said as he stood. "Now, let's go eat cake."

• • •

No matter how gorgeous a shirtless Will looked wielding a plate of equally tempting chocolate cake, Kory knew she should leave. She didn't want to blur the lines any more than they already were. She also didn't want to be embroiled in some idiotic competition over whether she stayed in Harmony Falls or went back to Chicago. There was no contest. Chicago would win. She'd worked too hard to get there.

Those thoughts clouded her mind enough she reached out and accepted the plate he was offering, only to regret it seconds later. Was she losing her sharp edge? That couldn't happen. And if it was, it was only happening because she had too much time on her hands. In Chicago she barely had time to breathe, let alone get mixed up with a man.

She should've given the plate of cake back, or set it down, and she tried, but her arm wouldn't cooperate. It seemed like such a shame to let good dessert go to waste. And the wine? Someone had to drink that, too.

Kory accepted the glass without protest. With her hands as full as her head, she settled on the couch, watching Will cut a piece of cake for himself. The thick, corded muscle in his forearm flexed as he slid the knife back and forth, and for a moment she just enjoyed the view, remembering how his muscles felt beneath her hands.

"Eat," he said, drawing her attention back to the cake on her plate. "Rumor has it this is the best cake in Harmony Falls. What do you think?"

As though she were in a trance, she raised a forkful to her mouth. Rich, cold fudge melted on her tongue, prompting an eye roll and whimper.

Will sat, grinning and adding to the decadent moment. "Lives up to its reputation, huh?"

She nodded. "Who made it?"

"You won't believe me," he said, chocolate kissing the corner of his mouth.

"You?"

"No. Probably even less believable. Charlie Cramer."

Kory set her fork on the plate and picked up the wine to wash down the sweetness along with her surprise. She was still getting used to Alice's brother providing this town with anything other than misery from his alcoholic past. "Wow."

"Yep. I want him to open a bakery on Main Street. He says he's not staying in Harmony Falls, but we'll see. I have a plan to convince him."

Interesting. Will was trying to convince Charlie Cramer to stay in Harmony Falls, too. Slowly, Kory's worried stomach settled. The reason Will wanted her to stay was clouded by the fact they were sleeping together, but after hearing she wasn't his lone pursuit, she was reminded this was about more than her—when it came down to it, Will's family mission to stabilize Harmony Falls' population and economic decline was his top priority.

They ate. Molly curled at their feet. It was a companionable silence, interrupted only by more thoughts. If Will ultimately wanted her in the name of Harmony Falls' success, then she was off the hook as far as affairs of the heart were concerned. She was also sure to win the non-existent challenge he'd accepted on the patio. Once the nursing home was in shape and she found a suitable replacement, he'd let her go without a second glance.

See? No worries, she thought, despite a fresh upset in her gut.

"You've got something right here," he said, touching his thumb to her bottom lip, but then he pulled away, set his plate on the coffee table, and slid closer. "On second thought…" He licked the spot where his thumb had been, and without hesitation, Kory set her plate aside, too, opening her mouth for his kiss.

Staying or leaving, she was here now. She wasn't going to waste this.

CHAPTER ELEVEN

Time *did* fly when Will was having fun, and Kory was his choice entertainment. Days turned to weeks with Will more and more convinced she needed to stay. But convincing her wasn't going to be easy.

He'd accepted a lot of personal and professional challenges in his high-achieving life, but throwing down the gauntlet where Kory and Chicago were concerned might have been his most foolish yet. Still, he couldn't back down. How would that look? Worse, how would that feel? He wanted her here for as long as he could keep her, which was foolish, too. No matter how many times he told himself it was good for business, it was even better for his personal life.

Will enjoyed her—in and out of bed, which was a novelty for him. While there was no shortage of women around town who wanted to sleep with a Mitchell, women who really understood him and enjoyed his company were rare.

He winced. *What the hell am I doing?*

Technically, it was called Operation Keep Kory or OKK for short. He dubbed it that one evening when he was overly tired and completely out of his mind. It involved little things, like staying out of her way at the nursing home, giving her the space he suspected she needed, and not talking about his growing admiration of her and confusing feelings. In return, she was easily and regularly crawling into his bed. When they weren't naked and otherwise engaged, they enjoyed each other's company, talking about her father's steady progress, the glimmers of hope in the nursing home budget and a love for watching mixed martial arts, of all things. Though Will supposed he shouldn't be that surprised that the ultra-competitive, no-holds-barred nature of the sport appealed to them both.

When she was with him in the evenings, lounging on his sofa with Molly tucked between them, his life felt full. He had to admit he'd thought once or twice about altering his poor outlook on relationships.

The thoughts always started the same way. Maybe he could make a relationship work? Wasn't it essentially what they had?

The thoughts always ended the same way, too. He was too old and jaded for a long-distance relationship, and long distance was what it would be…unless he could make her stay.

He glanced at his phone where his calendar read *2:30 P.M. Meeting with Charlie Cramer.* It had taken days to get Charlie to agree to this meeting, and Will still wasn't convinced the guy would show. But after eating a Charlie Cramer chocolate cake, Will had refused to give up. Maybe that was why he started to whistle when he spied Charlie already waiting for him across Main Street. That was a good sign.

Charlie's hands were buried in his jeans pockets. A bright tattoo covering his forearm attracted Will's attention. *That's new.* Sort of like Charlie Cramer, clean and sober, was new. Charlie Cramer, a brilliant baker and chef? Now, that was beyond new. That was brilliant, and Will was going to capitalize on it.

He hit the curb with pep in his step. "Thanks for meeting me."

Charlie reached out with the tattooed arm and gave Will's hand a hearty shake. "Why not? What have I got to lose by listening?"

"Smart man." Will smacked his back. "But the real question is what have you got to gain?" Turning him around by the shoulder, they faced the derelict building a few doors down from the gleaming Harmony Falls Little Theatre, whose marquee still proclaimed the happy news about Justin and Alice's wedding. "What do you think?"

"You don't want to know," Charlie said, shaking his head, hands still in his pockets.

"Come on. Use your imagination. Expect the same transformation your sister's theatre underwent."

Charlie looked in the direction of Alice's theatre and shook his head again. "That took tons of cash."

"Lucky for you, I know people with tons of cash who are interested in investing."

Will led him inside where they talked specifics. On more than one occasion, Charlie smiled with his eyes, giving away his enthusiasm. And by the end of the meeting, Will was feeling pretty good about Operation Keep Charlie, too.

"I can't make any promises." Charlie shoved his hands back into his pockets. "I'm waiting on some news. My whole life is going to depend on that."

Will knew the guy had demons, so he didn't press the cryptic reply. Instead, he thanked Charlie for meeting him and set up another to go over a potential timeline and business plan. In Charlie's words, what did he have to lose by listening?

With that squared away, Will moved on to the next thing on his list. "I have a favor to ask," he said as they stepped onto the sidewalk and into the sunshine. "What do you know about deep dish pizza?"

Charlie shrugged. "Not much."

"Could you make one?" Will asked, refusing to be deterred.

Charlie wrinkled his nose. "I can make anything."

"Good, then I want to hire you to cater a romantic dinner for two."

"With deep dish pizza on the menu?"

"Yep, also Chicago-style hot dogs."

"I'm sensing a theme here."

Definitely, but the theme wasn't "Chicago." No, the theme was "Everything you love about Chicago you can get here." Silly?

Probably. Overly simplistic? Absolutely. But it was all part of his grand plan, a plan that hinged on Valley Hospital.

Yesterday, Fran mentioned an expanded rehab unit and talk about a residency program. She'd heard word of it from a social worker friend. In Fran's eyes, that meant more patients in need of long-term care. In Will's eyes, that meant career opportunity beyond a rundown nursing home for Kory.

He wasn't stupid. He knew neither Harmony Falls nor Rileyville could compete head-to-head with Chicago as far as career advancement was concerned, but there had to be more to offer her than a part-time gig as a nursing home's resident physician. And if there was, maybe that something coupled with the other benefits of living in Harmony Falls, like being near her parents, her best friend…and dare he include him, would be enough to make her stay. *Maybe.*

It was a very big maybe.

"Can you handle the dinner?" Will asked.

"Absolutely," Charlie said without blinking. "Just let me know when you need me."

The exact date would depend on Valley. If the news was good and hospital administration sounded receptive to discussing opportunities with Kory, then dinner would serve as the perfect time to tell her.

Slipping behind the wheel of his car, Will whistled again while thoughts of Kory rolled around in his head. As much as he'd been staying away from her at work in the spirit of giving her space, he craved a break from that self-imposed rule today. Seeing her on the heels of a successful meeting was one way to make this day even better.

Five minutes later, he pulled into a parking spot at Harmony Elder Care as an ambulance rolled up alongside him. *Exit or entrance?* He hadn't heard a siren. Even so, he waited, watching from his car as the paramedics opened the double doors and used a lift to lower an occupied wheelchair. Will didn't recognize the street-clothed man.

Another new admission. He'd been keeping track of the numbers through Fran. Those extra hours Kory spent selling the patients and doctors at Valley Hospital on her merits and the merits of Harmony Falls Elder Care were paying off. But he didn't know just how well they were paying off until he stepped into the lobby and was accosted by Fran.

"Full," she mouthed. "We are full for the first time in three years." She might not be Dr. Flemming's biggest fan, but she had to admit this was impressive.

And for Will, it was all the more reason to keep Kory here.

• • •

Even though it wasn't something a doctor was expected to do, Kory coached her father through range of motion exercises. She lifted his arm over his head, bent his elbow, and opened and closed his hand. ESPN played on the suspended television overhead.

"Sanders got traded," Kory said, knowing that was one baseball player her father couldn't stand.

Dad nodded, the skin around his eyes crinkling.

"I bet you're happy about that."

"Ah am." The words were drawn out, but they sounded clearer every day. Or maybe Kory was just learning to understand him better.

She'd been spending a lot of her free time in here, trying to combat his depression. The sullen mood was to be expected, and she got to see firsthand how human interaction helped. When she was here, talking about things like Sanders, her father wasn't alone, thinking about things like never walking again. And sometimes, that mattered more to his recovery than all the physical therapy sessions in the world.

Later in the day, Kory watched as her father prepared to attempt his first steps without the aid of a hemi walker. They'd been working towards this for a week. Kory didn't know how she'd react if he failed. Hope strangled words of encouragement in her throat.

"Alright, Mr. Flemming. Let's get you up and walking." Bev tossed Kory a nervous smile as she helped him stand.

Really, it was amazing what positive progress could do. Bev heartily helping Kory with her father was inconceivable a few weeks ago.

And in the blink of an eye, her father was walking with assistance, but less assistance than before and without grumbles of pain.

"Naht bah for an ol mahn," he said.

Kory blinked away premature tears, reminding herself they still had so far to go. It was clearer than ever he wouldn't be roofing again, but he just might make it home.

"Not bad for an old man at all," she said smiling.

He made it down the hall and back again, just in time for Will to turn the corner up ahead.

Kory's eyes locked on the gorgeous man in the suit, and her pulse quickened. She'd seen him almost every night for the last week, but the familiarity didn't dull her excitement over seeing him again. It also didn't dull her worry over feeling that way, but she did a better job ignoring the worry than the excitement.

Will smiled at her, and then looked to her father. "What do we have here?"

Everyone was smiling now, and Kory only wished her mother wasn't out for a late lunch today. This was something to see.

After Bev helped Kory return her father to his bed, Kory hurried to her office where Will was waiting. She couldn't ever recall her heart feeling heavy in a good way, but it'd been happening a lot lately. She opened the door, stepped inside and found Will pushed back in her chair, feet resting on her desk.

"Make yourself comfortable why don't you?" She felt the goofy grin on her face.

"I'd be more comfortable with you on my lap." He patted his thigh in invitation.

She laughed. "No you wouldn't. That chair is missing a bolt, and if you sit off balance, it tips."

"Oh." He dropped his feet to the floor and stood, pressing palms to the desk. "How's this? Sturdy enough for two?" The desk shifted under the pressure. "Damn it. We need to get you usable furniture."

"It is usable. For appropriate office activities," she said, still laughing, head shaking.

He moved closer, backing her against the wall. "You mean this isn't an appropriate office activity?" Smoothing hands over her breasts to her neck, he dropped his mouth to hers and kissed her until the rest of the world fell away.

Seconds. Minutes. Hours. Who knew how much time passed before he abandoned her mouth and nuzzled her ear. "You make me feel like being inappropriate," he whispered.

She shuddered and dipped her fingers beneath the belted waistband of his dress pants. "Same here."

"Then I'm ordering you better furniture." He released her and stepped away, reaching for the closed door.

Kory stayed pressed against the wall, breathless and overheated. "You're leaving?"

"It was only supposed to be a quick stop. I have work to do. So do you. But I'll see you tonight." He winked as he opened the door and walked away.

Kory couldn't breathe. She clamped a hand around her throat and felt her heart beating there. What was he doing to her? This—whatever it was—was so much more than she wanted it to be.

Like the dork she was, she checked her pulse. She was still trying to count straight when her office door opened and Will walked back in.

"Screw it. I'll be late," he said, wrapping his arms around her.

And she made damn sure he was.

Afterwards, Kory's breathing refused to regulate. She went about her business, trying desperately not to worry about what was happening between them, but it wasn't easy. Every time she turned her head she smelled his fresh scent on her clothes, in her hair. She was obviously losing her mind, because hours later when she visited with a new admission, she tasted him on her lips. And driving home, with her mother sitting silently beside her, Kory could've sworn she heard his whisper on the wind.

Rolling up the window, she glanced at her mother. "What a day."

Mom nodded. "I'll make pork chops for dinner."

It was so random, Kory laughed.

"What's so funny about pork chops?"

"Nothing," Kory said, laughing harder.

The right side of Kory's face heated as she sensed her mother's stare. She was probably wigged-out by the laughter, worried it meant Kory was happy. Here. In Harmony Falls. Where she wasn't happy for some mysterious reason.

Kory bit back the laughter and waited for the lecture on returning to Chicago to begin.

"Thank you."

Kory snapped her head around so hard she nearly ran the truck off the road. "For what?"

"For giving me back the man I married. I heard him laugh today for the first time in weeks. Just like you are now."

Kory had blocked tears a few times today, but she couldn't block these ones. A fat one slipped down her cheek, and she brushed it away. "Well, he's not back yet. We still have a ways to go."

"Kory, look at me."

More tears fell, and she swiped her cheek again. "I can't. I'm driving."

Mom reached across the center seat and tugged Kory's right hand from the wheel. "The progress he's made is because of you. So from the bottom of my heart, thank you."

Kory held her breath, trying to prolong the unexpected, perfect moment. She felt wanted—needed—at home. All because of a laugh.

Mom didn't say much more, but she held tight to Kory's hand. As the silence dragged on, Kory's thoughts became more and more convoluted. She was happy before, wasn't she? Look at all she'd achieved on an elite and even national scale. How could she not be happy with that? But somehow, it didn't compare to this day's happiness. This day in Harmony Falls in a weathered—but at-capacity—nursing home with a bossy—but sexy—Will Mitchell and her imperfect—but supportive—parents by her side was…the happiest day of her life?

She squeezed her eyes shut and opened them quickly, refocusing on the road. No. She was tired. Overworked. Obsessed with her father's recovery and the home's bottom line. In this land of low-achievers and low-achievement, she was simply suffering from exaggerated joy at whatever remotely happy thing managed to occur despite her small town, dead-end surroundings.

Kory waited for that rationale to sink in. Waited for the relief. Instead she spent the rest of the ride home dodging hypothetical questions related to her staying in Harmony Falls.

That was not going to happen. Despite her mother's hand still warming hers. Despite her father's progress. Despite how far the home had come. Despite Will.

She should cancel on Will tonight. She couldn't cancel her parents. She couldn't cancel her job. But putting some distance between her and all of the warm, fuzzy, convoluted emotions she felt when she was with him was probably a good idea.

But the thought of actually following through and canceling on Will dulled her happiness, which seemed like such a shame. It had been a long, dark couple of months. Who could blame her for wanting to revel a little in her current happiness, even if that happiness was precariously built on a loosely packed hill of denial?

Nope. Kory refused to cancel. *Not yet*, she thought. One of these days, she would push Will away—but not today. Today had been too perfect.

CHAPTER TWELVE

As busy as Kory was at work and with the way she'd been carrying on with Will, Alice's return to Harmony Falls seemed rather sudden, but it was Will's invitation to go together to Mrs. Mitchell's welcome home party for the newlyweds that came out of nowhere.

With her fingers spread around the stem of her wine glass, Kory moved her hand in small circles against his patio table, swirling the glass, watching as it smeared condensation on the tabletop with every pass. "Are you asking me to go in general, or are you asking me to be your date?"

"If I say yes to the latter, will you say yes?"

She didn't have to look at him to know he was staring at her from across the table. If she looked up, she'd see the same handsome face she'd been looking at all evening. He'd be wearing a crooked smile that emphasized the cleft in his chin, and he'd be trying to use those wide, brown eyes to hypnotize her into doing whatever he wanted. Although she had given him some leeway in that department lately, this time, it wasn't going to happen.

Molly's collar jingled, but still Kory didn't look up. She refused to see Will's face when she took the first step toward pushing him away.

"No," she said, fighting a cringe. "Won't that just make things worse between you and your mother? Besides, we aren't dating. You know that. Dating implies we have a future." Her mouth felt tacky. She'd never had trouble speaking her mind before, but suddenly, for a split second, she wondered if she should continue. She wondered if there was a way to stop and take it back. A heartbeat later, she finished hard. "We don't have a future."

The backyard birds must have missed the stark announcement, because they continued their same perky songs, growing even louder. Somewhere in the distance a lawnmower purred. But Will didn't make a sound.

Curious, Kory looked up from her glass.

He lifted his beer bottle to his mouth and drank, his eyes never leaving her face.

"Did you see they canceled the McNeil fight?" he asked as if she hadn't said anything at all.

She almost took the bait and questioned him about the fight. Being stuck in Harmony Falls, working her butt off in an antiquated nursing home and living in a house without cable television, meant she hadn't heard anything yet. As much as she wanted to sit here, sipping her wine, talking about mixed martial arts and enjoying the view, she couldn't pretend she didn't just shoot Will down. After the way they'd been carrying on and his declaration that he accepted a stupid challenge she hadn't actually levied, she knew better than to think something like refusing to be his date could pass without him attempting to convince her again at some point.

This was Will Mitchell after all, and he didn't like to lose.

"Honestly, Will. I don't want Alice to know."

"About McNeil? I didn't know she was a fan."

Kory rolled her eyes. Sometimes he reminded her so much of the cocky kid from high school, chin lifted, shoulders back, like there wasn't a blow in the world that could hurt his pretty face. "You know what I'm talking about."

He exhaled long and loud. "Unfortunately, I do." When he reached underneath the table, his head disappeared for a second, and then he reappeared, tossing a raggedy stuffed animal into the yard.

Molly waddled after it.

"You're embarrassed of me," he said, nodding, a sly smile tipping his lips.

"Exactly." Her voice dripped with sarcasm. "But even more so, I don't want certain people making more out of this than there is. I'm not in the mood for speculative attention."

"Ooh. Big word, Dr. Flemming. Speculative." He raised his bottle again, eyeing her up, licking his lips. "Are you in the mood to follow me inside?"

Under different circumstances, she'd say yes, but Kory knew he wasn't really interested in sex as much as he was interested in diverting her. For a split second, she reveled in how well she knew him, how much easier their interactions were when she could predict his moves. Now that she saw beyond the bravado, she liked him. Admired him even. How could she fault him for traits like being determined and calculating? She was those things, too. They made for an interesting coupling—coupling being the operative word.

"We're not done with this conversation," she said, resolving to be every bit as determined as he was.

He chuckled. "You used to be so much easier to push around."

"That's not very nice," she said, narrowing her eyes, but knowing it was true.

"How about this then? I like it when you fight back. It's sexy." He grinned, and his white teeth sort of glowed in the evening sun.

"I'm pretty sure I should be offended by that statement," she said, but she was smiling, too.

"But you aren't."

No. A very short list of things offended her these days, and being called sexy by a man she couldn't quit certainly wasn't on that list. The fact that she couldn't quit him was more bothersome.

Kory looked at Molly, lounging in the middle of the yard, chewing on the stuffed toy. She started counting how many nights she'd been doing this, hanging out with Will and his dog. The camaraderie and comfort had become habit.

Habits were hard to break.

She sighed. "I don't want her to get her hopes up about this," Kory whispered.

So much dead silence stretched between them, she wondered if she'd said anything at all.

"Who?"

"Alice." It was a reasonable answer. Certainly more reasonable than admitting she was starting to worry about herself.

All these years of thinking she couldn't do a relationship, and here she was doing just about everything included in one, except calling it a relationship. Maybe she wasn't as much of a loner as she thought. Still, it was pointless even thinking about it, because there was no future here. If Will lived in Chicago…maybe. But he didn't. The heaviness in her chest made her slouch.

Will's chair creaked as he leaned forward and his hand smoothed over her bare thigh. When his fingers slipped beneath the hem of her shorts, she decided diversion was better than continuing with this conversation.

"If it makes you feel better, I'll ignore you at the party," he said. "But one way or another, you should be there for Alice."

The slight sweeps of his fingers against her inner thigh had her weak with tingles. She set her wine glass down rather than spill it, eager to get her hands on him instead. "Thank you."

"But you're going to have to give me your undivided attention now."

Doable. Very doable. She ran a hand up his arm and slipped her fingers beneath his sleeve. "Sounds like a fair trade."

It was as long as he held up his end of the deal.

• • •

Will watched Kory chat with Alice and the other bridesmaids from across the pool. He stayed true to his word, ignoring her so far, but it wasn't easy. A brown dress, shaped like an extra-long tank top hugged her subtle curves. Each side of the dress sported a generous slit from ankle to knee. And all he really wanted to do was sidle up to her, slip an arm around her waist and enjoy the evening by her side.

But he would be good. He promised.

Snatching a toothpick full of olives from the poolside bar, he munched as he mingled. Every few minutes he stole another glance at Kory. He tried not to let her grim outlook on their future bother him. After all, he didn't expect her to give serious credence to staying in Harmony Falls until she had a reasonably compelling job offer. But hearing her proclaim they had no future wounded him more than he cared to admit. He asked himself why a hundred times. After all, he never thought himself capable of a future that included the same woman, year after year, before. He also never realized he could enjoy someone the way he enjoyed Kory. Surely, she had to see how good they were together. It pained him even more to know being good together wasn't enough to make her stay.

He made his way to the same side of the pool as Kory, keeping a respectful distance as she chatted with Mark.

"Will Mitchell, you can sing?" He turned to see his sister-in-law open-mouthed, hands on hips. Several pairs of laughing eyes, including Kory's, were on him.

"I mean, I knew you liked opera, but you can sing it?" Alice continued, incredulously. "You have to sing for me, and then you have to audition for a show."

One set of laughing eyes belonged to Mark, who no doubt fed the group the embarrassing information.

"He's exaggerating, Alice. I don't sing."

Mark waved him off. "I've heard you."

"In the shower, when I was ten."

"He was singing Puccini."

Mark wasn't backing down, so Will stepped closer to the group, hoping to end the silliness. "And poorly I might add."

"Sing for us, Will?" Alice grabbed hold of his arm and dragged him into the circle of women.

He shook his head. He couldn't think of a more unpleasant situation to be in. Having grown up on his parent's love of opera, he had a deep appreciation for the music. And yes, he sang from time to time. But he didn't pretend to be any good. Certainly, he wasn't good enough to sing for other people.

"No, Alice. Not a chance."

"He's scared." The voice surprised him. He looked at Kory, who was smiling. "He's afraid he won't be any good."

There was an unspoken challenge in her eyes.

She wanted him to sing? She wanted him to fail? Which was it? He found himself chuckling, unsure of her motive or why the goading had him considering his options. He could refuse, walk away and give her the satisfaction of believing she was right, and he was scared. Or he could sing and, even if he sucked, prove her wrong.

She was still smiling, eyes locked with his. It was the closest they'd been all night, and the connection was heady, stirring desire in his gut and causing a buzz in his mouth. He started singing without thought. Just a few lines really, nothing too loud or compelling. He sang to her, only to her, loving the way her smile faltered and her eyes widened as she welcomed him in. Time and place slipped away. If he'd been thinking straight, he could've anticipated the magnitude of the silence surrounding them when he finished. As it was, he didn't get it until Justin intervened.

"Show off."

Will snapped out of the trance to look at his older brother who must've come closer during the mini-performance.

"Nah, just proving a point," Will said, careful not to look at Kory, certain every other woman in that circle was wondering what was going on between them.

"I'm putting 'Pirates of Penzance' on the schedule," Alice said, and then she grabbed Kory's hand. "I have to go to the ladies' room. Come with me."

He watched them walk away.

"What is it with women always going in pairs?" Justin asked. "Do they really need to pee in unison?"

Will had a feeling Alice and Kory's rapid retreat had nothing to do with their bladders.

• • •

"What's going on with you and Will?" Alice asked the minute the bathroom door shut behind them.

Kory had to give Alice credit. At least she got right to the point. The minute Will's mouth had closed Kory knew she'd be doing damage control. Actually, she knew it the minute his mouth opened and he started singing. *To her.* She melted despite knowing everyone else was watching the strangely intimate moment. Being dragged through a large house to the bathroom gave Kory just enough time to prepare a response, but on the heels of Alice's directness it seemed insulting to give her anything less in return.

"We've been hanging out."

"I knew it," Alice hissed. "You like each other. Don't deny it."

"It's just for fun."

"Whatever was going on out there wasn't just for fun. That was the most romantic thing I've ever seen, and you two have a serious connection." Alice gasped. "Are you sleeping together?"

Kory heard the question, but she was hung up on the words "romantic" and "serious connection." Will singing to her had felt that way, too. Over the last several weeks she'd gone from enjoying his company to adoring him beyond reason. And there were witnesses. She looked away, hoping for some semblance of peace to decide what to say next.

Alice pounced on the silence. "You *are* sleeping together. I can't believe you didn't tell me. My best friend is sleeping with my brother-in-law, and she didn't tell me." She threw up her hands.

Kory squirmed. "It's not a big deal, Alice. I'm still going back to Chicago…soon. Real soon." The words were lame. They lacked power and punch.

Alice's nose wrinkled as she studied Kory. "I know that."

It was hot in the bathroom. Too hot. Kory felt her face flush, and she blew a little puff of air over her upper lip. "Good. I just want to make sure it's clear."

Alice gripped Kory's hand and squeezed. "Aw, honey, now I'm worried the only one who isn't clear on it is you."

Kory didn't like feeling annoyed with Alice, but she was, and rather than stay here, dealing with those feelings on top of facing Will again, she decided to leave, knowing her early departure would cause even more questions. Fortunately, Mrs. Mitchell was lingering in the kitchen, so Kory was able to say a proper thank you and goodbye to her hostess before she bolted. But that didn't assuage her guilt over leaving without saying goodbye to Will. She couldn't help but wonder what he would think when he figured out she wasn't returning. She hoped he wasn't too disappointed, hoped he didn't take it too personally. This was about her not him. Alice was right. Kory needed clarity, and she wasn't going to find it hypnotized by Will.

The ride home was long and laborious, with Kory's thoughts pummeling her brain until she had a first-rate headache. When Kory pulled in a little after nine, Aunt Jeanie's car was in the driveway. Knowing Aunt Jeanie normally dropped her sister off on the fly, the parked, empty car concerned Kory. But then the concern turned to annoyance. She really didn't want to explain her early departure from the party.

Stopping far enough behind to allow Aunt Jeanie plenty of room to back out and around her, Kory crawled out of the truck with her cell phone in hand, figuring she could feign some work emergency if need be. She walked. The dogs didn't greet her, which was odd, unless they were off hunting small, defenseless animals again. Something just didn't seem right, and she slowed her steps, moving silently onto the porch and opening the screen door.

Holding her breath, she stepped inside and stopped, waiting for the dogs again. Nobody welcomed her. No television noise filled the front room. Just when she was ready to panic, she heard voices from the kitchen, and relief set in.

She stepped forward again.

"Some days I think it would be best to tell her the truth, but how do you tell someone she was almost aborted."

It was her mother's voice. The vague collection of words eradicated the relief and gave way to a painful twisting in Kory's gut. *Who* was almost aborted?

"I still say no. What good could come of Kory knowing?"

Kory. She doubled over, grabbing hold of her stomach. Abortion was such a harsh word, and an even harsher action.

Thumping and barking hit her from behind as the dogs jumped onto the porch, greeting her through the screen, rattling the wood pane with their paws.

"Is someone there?" Mom called, her voice growing louder and closer with every syllable.

Kory didn't want to be found. She wanted time to process this.

"Oh...I...why are you here?" The last part was so high-pitched that it made Kory wince.

She squeezed her eyes shut before she opened them and looked at her mother, not knowing if she had the strength to say the words forming in her head. Breathing felt like stabbing to her chest, but she did it anyway—did it so she could say, "Maybe that's a question I should be asking you. If you wanted to abort me, then why am I here?"

"You heard." Mom went pale, tears rolled from her eyes, and she opened her arms to Kory. "I'm so sorry. I…"

Kory stepped back just as Aunt Jeanie walked into the room. "Baby girl, let her explain."

Shock. Bone-deep sadness. It settled over Kory like a thick fog that dulled her senses, threatening to pull her to the ground.

"Kory, listen to me. I love you."

Parents loved their children, of course. But this…this changed things. "You *love* me, but you didn't want me." She said the words, trying to clarify their meaning, trying to reconcile how one could exist with the other. *Just have this conversation and get past it*, Kory thought, trying to maintain a death grip on her composure. She was too old, too worldly to not understand people had their reasons. She'd heard many of them during her obstetrical rotations in medical school. She just never imagined she'd be hearing one that pertained to her.

"We didn't know what we wanted. I went to the clinic, because I didn't think I had a choice. Your father was accepted into an architecture program in Michigan. It was his dream, but it was a fulltime program, and I couldn't imagine him succeeding if he worked, too. So I was going to carry us, but I didn't have a skill beyond waitressing. We had a thousand dollars of wedding gift money to our name, and we hoped that was enough to find an efficiency and get us to Michigan so I could find work. When I found out I was pregnant, we were in shock. How would we add a baby to that? How would we afford daycare?"

It was a tough predicament to be in. Newly married, ready to conquer their dreams, and then… standing there, listening to her mother's sniveling words, Kory felt oddly removed, like the story wasn't one that almost ended with her not being here.

"I wanted your father to have everything he ever dreamed of, so I told myself it was the smart thing to do. He could concentrate on school, and I could work to pay the bills, and we'd have more children when the time was right. It was an initial instinct, but we couldn't go through with it." Mom grabbed Kory's hand. "I'm so glad I didn't. I adore you. You are everything to us. That's why we'll stop at nothing to see you succeed. Please, Kory, don't let this upset you." She placed a hand on Kory's cheek, and Kory dutifully nodded. All the years of parental pride over her achievements and pressure to be gone in order to achieve more. They all made sense now. Her parents chose her over their dreams of getting out of Harmony Falls, and they weren't going to let her do the same.

It was too much to process. Too confusing to make real sense of it now. Except, maybe sacrifice was the greatest kind of love.

Clarity. Kory left the Mitchell's house in search of it, and boy did she find it.

Chicago was where she belonged.

CHAPTER THIRTEEN

When Kory didn't return to the party, Will suspected she was mad. He never intended the little performance to tip off anyone about the relationship neither one of them was comfortable claiming just yet. But apparently he'd made it loud and clear, because Alice returned to the party, treating him with extra kindness and aiming many inquisitive glances his way. He didn't think her attention had anything to do with her wanting him to sing again.

On the way home, he thought about calling Kory, apologizing for making a spectacle out of them, but he figured she wouldn't answer if she was mad—look what happened when he called back after the butt dial. Stopping by her house wasn't wise, either. She wouldn't be alone, and cluing her mother into the something brewing between them was bound to make Kory even angrier. So, he drove home and let himself into the darkened house, where he attempted to take solace in Molly's warm greeting.

Still the house felt empty, and he woke up feeling like he hadn't slept at all.

At a quarter after nine the next morning, his cell phone rang. Dr. Don Waterman listened while Will praised Kory, and eventually the man agreed to consider her for the Valley Hospital residency program directorship. All she had to do was forward him her *curriculum vitae*.

Will winced, convincing Kory of that would take more than Chicago-style deep-dish pizza and hot dogs after last night. Still, he had a plan and a chef on standby. So he called Charlie and charged ahead.

After a morning of meetings, Will decided enough was enough, and he dialed her. She didn't answer. A little anxious that his big evening could go down without a dinner guest, he drove over to the nursing home during an afternoon lull. She wasn't in her office, so he wandered down the hall to her father's room.

"Afternoon, Mr. Flemming, Mrs. Flemming," Will said, poking his head around the doorjamb for a quick look. No Kory there either.

Ken lifted his good hand to wave.

"Hello, Will," Carole said, a blank expression on her face.

She looked tired, even more tired than him. He supposed that was the byproduct of worry and hours spent shut inside a nursing home. Again, he admired Kory's self-sacrifice in order to get her father home and her parents back to some semblance of normal.

Feeling it would be rude to leave after a quick hello, he walked into the room with a smile. "You're looking stronger every day, Mr. Flemming. You'll be home in no time." He patted the man's leg.

Ken laughed. "I feel good." The words were slow and broken, but all the parts were there for him to be understood.

Will remembered when nothing the man said sounded remotely familiar. It had to thrill Kory to see the progress.

Will patted him again. "How's our resident doctor treating you? She better not be pushing you too hard."

It was a joke, but no one laughed. The Flemmings exchanged rigid glances, and then Ken grunted. "I feel good," he said again.

The whole exchange seemed strange, and in that moment Will felt terribly unwelcomed. He smiled to hide his confusion over whatever was happening. "Good. Good to hear. Well, I'll let you get your rest. Mrs. Flemming." He tipped his head as he backed away.

She curved her lips, but it was hardly a smile.

An unsettled feeling accompanied Will through the halls as he wandered around in search of Kory, but she was nowhere to be found. Finally, Bev asked him if he was looking for something.

"Have you seen Dr. Flemming?"

Her brows lifted. "Not since this morning. She rounded early and in a hurry, and she left before ten."

It was one more thing to make him uncomfortable.

"Is she over at Valley schmoozing social workers and families, drumming up more admissions?"

Bev shook her head. "Nope. She went yesterday. She only does that once a week."

Maybe she was home. Will glanced at his watch, knowing he had too little time between now and his two-o'clock meeting to drive out to the Flemming house. Then it dawned on him she might be with Alice, and the possibility took some of the edge off. He dialed her number again when he reached his car.

"I was just about to call you." Kory's voice was dulled by a whooshing sound that made it hard to hear her and impossible for him to be as happy about talking to her as he hoped to be.

"Where are you? You sound like you're in a wind tunnel."

"Driving. Windows are down. Listen, we need to talk. Tonight."

"Yes. Good. My house. Say seven?"

"I'll see you there."

"Kory…" He wasn't going to let her hang up and relegate him to the rest of the day worrying about where they stood. "Are you mad at me?"

The whooshing threatened to drown her out. "No. I'll see you tonight."

Silence settled over him as the line went dead. She wasn't mad, and he would see her tonight. So why didn't he feel any better?

• • •

Kory glanced at the papers on the passenger seat. They were held in place despite the whipping wind with the weight of her purse. Finding an attorney who would look over her employment contract on such short notice wasn't easy. She had to drive two towns past Rileyville and miss her father's morning physical therapy session, but she kept telling herself peace of mind was worth the hassle. She needed to know what she'd be up against when she handed Will her resignation tonight.

He wouldn't be happy. In fact, she was preparing for livid, and if she wanted to get to Chicago to rejoin her fellowship program by the end of next week, she needed him not to fight her leaving. Now that she knew there was very little he could do to enforce the breach of contract, which would result from her not giving thirty-day notice like the contract stated, she was breathing a little easier. A little. Her lungs still burned. She wasn't the kind of person who liked leaving anyone in a lurch, and leaving with limited notice was bound to cause a problem for the nursing home.

This was not how she hoped to leave Harmony Falls, but last night changed everything.

Slowing her speed as she entered town, Kory contemplated returning to the nursing home, checking in with her parents to see how her father's session went, but a thickening thread of self-preservation told her to stay away, let them get used to her not being around, let her get used to it, too.

This morning when Kory announced she was returning to Chicago, her mother wasn't nearly as relieved as Kory anticipated she would be. Oh, she said she was, adding *that's where you belong* to the conversation more than once, but there wasn't any excitement. Kory refused to let that sway her. It was probably just emotional exhaustion from the upheaval of the stroke and the admission of a secret carried far too long.

A bubble of stomach acid pushed into Kory's throat and popped in her mouth. She'd been battling the upset since last night. What her parents did or didn't do almost thirty years ago didn't matter. What mattered was what they did now. This morning when she walked into her father's room mid-rounds, she could tell by the look on her mother's face he was apprised of the situation. Still, he smiled and gripped her right hand so hard a bruise remained on her finger from the pressure of her ring.

"I love you more than life itself," he'd said, despite the struggle of tears on top of dysarthria.

See? It wasn't that she wasn't wanted; they simply wanted more for her. Call it living vicariously. Call it warped retribution. She was thankful for whatever it was.

Alice's theatre came into view, and Kory needed to see her, and not just to tell her she was leaving. So many times over the years when things were particularly hard being out on her own, she'd wished for the luxury of walking into Alice's house, where whatever chaos was occurring was bound to make her feel better about her own. Before too long, she'd be back in that predicament again.

When Kory stepped inside the overly air-conditioned, glitzy lobby, she could smell Alice's perfume, and the scent made her smile. It was funny how a person could put her stamp on a neutral space. It was a business, not Alice's house, but it *felt* like Alice.

The double doors to the theatre swung open and Alice's assistant, Wren Cannon, stopped them mid-swing. "Hey, you. What a nice surprise. You came to help us catalog the costume room, didn't you?"

Kory laughed and pointed to Wren's head. "Is that why you're wearing horns?"

She stepped forward, letting the doors swing shut with a soft thud and pulled the item in question in front of her face, dragging along with it several strands of orange hair. "They are for the youth theatre production of 'How to Train Your Dragon'. Cute, huh? I swear to God, playing around in the costume room is the best part of my job." She slapped the horns back on her head. "Come on, you can help me carry a few more boxes up. Alice will be so happy to see you."

An hour later, Kory was ankle deep in toile and sporting a purple feather boa, and somehow against all odds she was having a good time.

"How about this one?" Wren asked, holding up a red velvet cape.

"Little Red Riding Hood," Alice said, scribbling in the binder perched on her lap. "*Into the Woods.*"

Wren whipped the cape around her back, adding it to her strange Viking ensemble. "If I'd have had this collection in high school, I'd have been legendary."

Kory chuckled, because Wren was already legendary. There wasn't another girl in their graduating class whose prom dress had been made out of duct tape.

"Do you ever take this stuff home and wear it for...?" Wren whistled.

Alice looked up, blinking, her expression innocent enough, but Kory knew better.

"Maybe," Alice said.

Kory smirked. "Of course she does."

Wren bobbed her bushy brows.

All three of them burst into laughter.

"And now that I have money, they are dry-cleaned thoroughly before they're returned," Alice said.

The laughter stopped, giving way to *ewww*'s.

"T.M.I." Wren removed the cape, but kept the horns.

Alice waved away the concerns. "Oh, grow up. I don't wear the stuff during...you know."

A buzzer sounded overhead. "Probably mail," Wren said, moving toward the door. "Be right back."

Alice continued to lift items from the pile at her feet and scribble in her binder while Wren's platform heels clanged against the metal steps, growing quieter and quieter. When the sound disappeared, the pen stopped moving.

"Is everything okay between you and Will?" Alice asked.

Kory bent forward and picked up a poodle skirt, running her hand over the fuzzy applique. She knew the questions would start sooner or later. Wren being here only prolonged the inevitable conversation. But Kory wasn't here to talk about Will. That would only complicate a situation that was already way too complicated.

"I'm leaving," Kory announced. Quicker seemed less painful.

"When?"

"Next week."

"Why?"

"It's time."

"Kory, look at me."

It was harder than she expected it to be. And even after she looked up, she couldn't hold Alice's bright blue gaze for fear of doing something stupid, like crying without a good reason.

"Is it because of Will?"

Kory shook her head, swallowing down the strange brew of emotions, threatening her composure. "No. Chicago is where I belong."

And then Alice was beside her, sitting on the same plastic container, arm around her shoulders, opposite hand smoothing her leg. "You know, I could argue that."

"I'm sure you could."

There was so much comfort in being here with her. Neither one of them had a sister. This was as close as they would get. Maybe it was even better. They didn't share a family, so they could help each other keep family drama in perspective.

"Did you know my father wanted to be an architect?" Of course Alice didn't know, but Kory asked it all the same, unable to control the urge to tell Alice everything.

"No, but I could see him doing that. He loves construction."

Kory nodded. But construction wasn't the same as architecture. Repairing and replacing roofs wasn't sketching the Space Needle.

She wondered where he'd be now if… "They got pregnant with me, so he didn't go to architecture school. Isn't that sad?"

"No," Alice said, squeezing Kory against her chest. "I say they created something even better than a cold, hard building."

"They thought about aborting me." There. She said it. It hurt much less than she feared it would, which was good. Maybe that was what she was trying to prove by initiating this conversation in the first place. She still had control of the situation, control of her feelings.

Alice's silence was thick, but quick, and then she squeezed Kory again, adding, "I'm glad they didn't."

For some warped reason, that made Kory laugh. "Me, too."

This time, the silence was more comfortable, and lasted longer, long enough for Alice to drop her head to Kory's shoulder for a few shared breaths.

"Are you mad or sad about it?" Alice finally asked.

"Neither. I'm surprised. Who wouldn't be? But it explains a lot, why they always were so determined that I succeed. It makes me want to work even harder. For them." Alice leaned forward, and Kory felt the weight of her stare. "For me, too."

"Is that even possible? You already work so hard. Don't you ever get tired of it?"

Kory balked. "No." Which was a lie. The pace she kept in Chicago left her downright exhausted. She did get tired of moving from point A to point B in a blur. But all she'd ever wanted was to become a doctor in a major city at a world-class hospital. Complaining about achieving it was absurd.

"You are super human."

Nah. She was just doing what she planned to do. Her father was the one who was super human, suffering a major stroke and losing life as he knew it, but still finding reason to smile. Emotions knotted in Kory's chest, and she looked away before Alice could see the beginnings of tears. Leaving him, letting go of his care, was going to be the hardest part of leave Harmony Falls.

The clanging of Wren's heels up the metal steps couldn't have come at a better time.

With one more squeeze and a pat to Kory's back, Alice stood. "I support you in whatever you do. You know that. But I'm going to miss you," she said.

I'll miss you, too, Kory thought, but she couldn't say the words, not if she wanted to get out of town without looking back. There were already enough hurdles.

And she was sick to her stomach thinking about dealing with the biggest one tonight.

CHAPTER FOURTEEN

Will stood in the quiet kitchen, Molly at his side, knowing music would quell his nerves, but Kory might not appreciate his usual selections after last night. He passed on the opera and paced in silence instead.

The hot, spicy aromas of pepperoni, sausage, and onions filled the air, making his stomach grumble, but he didn't dare take the smallest bite. He suspected the minute anything solid hit the quivering muscle he'd puke. Nervous didn't begin to cut it. Hands sweaty, mouth dry, one would've thought he was getting ready to propose marriage.

His heart suddenly raced as his brain flashed a random scene of him sliding a ring onto Kory's finger. He was getting ahead of himself, and he needed to sit. The nerves and hunger were obviously wearing him thin.

Falling into the nearest chair, Will snagged a deli chip from a bowl and forced himself to eat it. Marriage was not on his agenda, and it wasn't on Kory's either. He liked her, more than he ever expected to like anyone, but marriage required love, the kind that made people ignore the pain that came from investing everything they had into one measly thing. He wasn't capable of that. He was a businessman. Diversification was how he succeeded.

Then why do you want her to stay? He looked at Molly as if she'd proposed the question, knowing full well it was the voice in his head. He grabbed another chip, trying to ignore it, but the words kept pushing their way to the forefront of his mind.

He thought while he chewed.

"I want her to stay, because I like spending time with her. I feel less lonely when she's around."

Molly whimpered.

Will reached out, offering her a chip as consolation. "You keep me company, too, but it's a different kind of company."

Memories of the last time Kory kept him company bombarded him. His face heated along with a stirring below his belt. He'd certainly miss *that* kind of company with Kory gone. It had been a long time since he had regular sex. Nodding, he reached for another chip. Aside from her success at the nursing home, that had to be the main reason he was so hell bent on making her stay.

He sat with the thought for a minute, expecting it to calm his nerves, because if he failed to keep her here and he managed to find a competent replacement medical director, then he could move on with his life pretty easily. Couldn't he? His leg bounced frantically, and in short order he'd polished off the whole bowl of chips.

"Shit," he murmured, standing and crossing the kitchen to refill the stainless steel bowl with whatever crumbs of deli chips remained in the opened bag.

The doorbell sounded, giving him a jolt, and when Molly barked a reply, Will's nerves shattered. "Quiet," he snapped, and then immediately wished it back.

The dog stared at him with droopy, dark eyes, the kind that said she was sorry for angering him. *Stupid*, he thought, dropping to his knees and pulling her close.

"You're a good girl." And maybe she would be his only girl by the end of the evening. He better not forget it.

Molly licked his cheek.

Together, they walked to the door and let Kory in.

• • •

It took Will so long to answer the door, Kory almost turned around. But she refused to add the word "coward" to her resume.

Giving him notice, even if it wasn't the lengthy notice he required, was the right thing to do.

She'd planned a speech of sorts. She knew what she wanted to say. But the minute he opened the door and smiled at her, all thought wiped away.

"Hey, you," he said, pausing for a moment to take her in before he stepped back and swung open the door.

She purposefully hadn't primped for the evening, not that Kory was the primping kind. Somehow she felt better driving over here in the business-casual clothes she'd worn to work and the attorney's office—without a brush to her hair or makeup on her face. But the way Will looked at her, she knew it didn't matter one bit to him what she was wearing. He was just happy to see her.

Her stomach lurched.

She nodded, and attempted to return his smile as she walked into the house. It felt fake, insulting even. Why would she smile at him when she knew the words she was about to say would upset him?

"Listen, about last night at the party." He closed the door and faced her.

Kory shook her head. The party seemed like a distant memory, considering all that had happened since.

"Let's not look back, Will." She couldn't. She wouldn't.

He stared at her, an inquisitive tilt to his head, and then he smiled again, rubbing his hands together. "Okay, then let's look ahead. Come here."

With a hitch of his index finger he urged her to follow, and despite the warning in her head, she did. In all her mental run-throughs of this meeting, she imagined delivering the news in his living room, and then leaving on a tsunami of his anger and hurt. Maybe even being thrown out. She didn't expect...

Dinner spread over the farmhouse table in his kitchen.

"I thought about setting up in the dining room, but that seemed too formal for what's being served."

The spicy scent of pizza nipped the lining of her nose. Her mouth watered, and she stepped closer for a better look.

It was a strange array of food. Deli chips… Hot dogs… Italian beef sandwiches… Her gaze snapped back to the deep-dish pizza in the center of the table. *Chicago.* She didn't think it was an accident the menu and location were related. She just couldn't understand why. Did he know she was returning to Chicago in a matter of days? Was this some twisted punishment meant to trump her announcement?

Kory exhaled. "I don't understand."

Will's smile was shaky. "Yeah. I was afraid of that. It seems incredibly stupid now." He roughed his face in his hands. "Okay, so here goes." He leveled her with warm brown eyes. "Everything Chicago has to offer you, I can offer you right here. The food, the friendships, the job opportunities." He stopped, opened his mouth and inhaled, nodding as he did, like he was reaffirming everything he said while he waited for her to agree.

But Kory was speechless, and her hands were trembling as she watched him turn to tug a manila envelope from beneath a plate. "Valley is starting a physical medicine residency program, and you've been invited to apply for the directorship." He offered a quick smile as he fanned the envelope in the space between them. "Go ahead. Take it. Read it. I think you'll be impressed with what they're trying to do."

Check mate.

An ice-cold nausea chilled her bones, freezing her hands to her sides. This was part of the challenge to make her stay, wasn't it? Somehow Will found out she was leaving and he prepared all of this as his last, desperate move. She did a quick mental rundown of everyone she'd spoken to: her parents, her fellowship director, the attorney, Alice. She couldn't imagine any of those people betraying her confidence.

Again the envelope waved, taunting her. And then worse, a quiet thought entered her head. Maybe he was asking her to stay simply because he wanted her to stay—because he wanted her.

A shaky exhale rushed across her lips. She'd waited a lifetime to be wanted like that. Of course, it would happen now, when the timing was all wrong, and there was nothing she could do about it. She belonged in Chicago. No matter what Will's intentions were or what the contents of his envelope said.

Shaking her head, Kory refused the envelope. "I can't, Will. You know I can't."

"How do you know you can't? You haven't even looked at it." When she didn't whisper a word let alone move a muscle to take the information, he smacked the envelope against the palm of his hand and sighed. "Let's eat. The food is getting cold."

He sat. It was a good thing, because if he didn't already know her resignation was coming, he was about to find out.

Kory wrung her hands and choked down a mouthful of air. "I'm resigning, Will. Effective immediately."

His hand, lifting a spatula loaded with stringy-cheese pizza, dripping pepperoni and sausage stopped mid-air. He didn't move. His stillness added to the quiet in the room until Molly's soft snoring was all Kory could hear. She never thought she would miss the ominous opera background noise that played like a soundtrack in his office but she did.

"I'm returning to Chicago in one week," she said.

He set the spatula on the table, and then he looked at her through narrowed eyes. The lips she'd enjoyed almost every evening for the last two months twisted.

"You agreed to give me thirty days' notice." The words were slow, calm, but exceedingly grim.

She was prepared for him to be upset. After all, he was a businessman who'd just been handed unexpected news that would negatively impact his bottom line. But preparing for ugliness and facing it were two very different things.

Opening her mouth for a quick, shaky breath, Kory forged ahead with a portion of the planned speech. "I know, and I apologize, but something came up, and I don't have a choice. I have to leave as soon as possible."

"What came up?" His eyes relaxed a little as he nodded. "Seriously, Kory, what came up? I'm a reasonable man. You should know that by now."

She found herself nodding, too. "I know you are, Will. I do, but..."—in her rush and worry she hadn't expected him to want more of an explanation. She figured her announcement would pretty much get her kicked out of his life for the rest of hers— "... it's personal."

His lips twisted again, and he made a laugh-like sound. "Personal. Too personal for me. Even though we've been on very personal terms."

She winced. He was right, of course. They'd been sharing some pretty personal thoughts and feelings over the last two months, but telling him about her mother's revelation seemed to go too far. If she let him in on the most intimate details of her life, then how would she shut him out?

Her heart ached.

"Maybe painful would be a better word." Though that didn't quite fit, either. "It's uncomfortable, Will. Please, leave it at that."

He stood, surprising her with hands to her shoulders and fingers resting on her neck. And when his face softened, she nearly crumbled.

"How am I supposed to ignore something that's causing you pain, especially when it's taking you away?"

As her heart throbbed, pressure mounted in her head, making it hard to formulate a reasonable answer. She'd never been an emotional person, and stress was something she steamrolled. Had two measly months in Harmony Falls really changed that?

"I belong in Chicago," she said. Trying so damn hard not to choke on the words, she did it anyway.

"So you say." His hands slid to the sides of her neck, and his thumbs traced her jaw. Back and forth. Back and forth. Until she closed her eyes.

"I owe it to my parents."

His lips brushed hers, and her heart stopped. "And what do you owe to yourself?"

She captured his upper lip between her lips for the smallest taste. This was not happening to her. Will Mitchell was not supposed to be a choice—at least not a legitimate one. But in his arms, under his spell, a part of her wanted to stay. A big part. A reckless part.

She pushed him away. "It's not about me, Will. It's about sacrifice and love so deep you give up what you want for the life and love of someone else."

• • •

Will could see the magnitude of this decision written all over Kory's drawn face, like he tasted it a moment ago in her desperate nip of a kiss. Wrinkles of concern tightened his forehead and flared his nostrils. If only he could fix whatever was pushing her away. He rubbed a palm over his heart, bunching his cotton shirt. The rustling noise echoed in the silence between them.

"And you're sure there's no other way?"

She looked at him for what seemed like the longest time, and like an idiot he prayed she'd figure out some way to stay.

"I have to go. I want to go." And yet her head hung. "This isn't some high school game you can win, Will."

The words hurt, and though he didn't want to hear them said, he expected them. Even though he'd hoped they'd come far enough to erase his earlier transgression, he knew they'd always be a part of him.

He took an impulsive step toward her, and when she didn't back away, he swept her into his arms, cradling her head to his heart.

For some reason, she felt she owed her life to her parents. If he didn't know the pressure of family expectations, if he didn't know the responsibility he'd been born into and how it governed the decisions he made each day, he could fight harder to make her stay. He might not know the details, but he understood her ambition and sense of obligation. He admired it.

"Go," he whispered into her sweet-smelling hair. Will realized he could be holding her like this for the last time, and he squeezed his eyes shut on a wave of regret. "I won't stand in your way." He wanted to, but he couldn't imagine being an added burden. She already looked ready to break.

Again he wondered what was so painful and uncomfortable she couldn't share it with him, but then her warm hands pushed beneath his shirt and fused against his back as she lifted her head and nuzzled him cheek to cheek. It was the single most depressing and yet enticing moment of his life. It was also cruelly ironic that at the moment he let her go, he was recognizing their relationship had changed and deepened enough to become something vital to him.

He covered her mouth with his, holding her head in place with hands pressed to either side of her face, while Kory slid her hands to his stomach, splaying her fingers as they climbed his body. Something about the way she touched him left him raw and burning. He lifted her face into the kiss, probing deeper into her mouth, mixing his tongue with hers, praying for a reprieve from all the hurt.

On the next beat of his heart he dropped his hands from her face and wound his arms around her waist, pressing her body to his, straddling her feet with his feet, backing her into the living room. The sound of her breathing echoed in his ears, stirring his desire. Her hands clawed his chest and into his sleeves, urging his arms up. After a series of harsh, breathless tugs, she ripped the shirt from his body.

His heart thrashed against his ribs, its overactive rate making him woozy. Then again, maybe the lightheadedness was because of the way she looked at him, really looked at him. He felt so transparent he had to blink. And then she grabbed him by the waistband of his shorts and turned him toward the couch. He sat before she asked him to and before she could push him down. He might as well maintain control of his actions as long as he could. He had a feeling it wouldn't be much longer now.

Kory didn't say a word as she kicked off her heels and stepped out of her pants. He rolled his gaze over long creamy legs to the flicker of white lace peeking at him from the split-hem of her blouse. When he looked at her face, she held his gaze with a warning gleam in her eyes. Somehow he knew if he didn't follow her lead, she'd make him comply—none-too-gently.

That was fine with him. He wasn't in the mood for gentle tonight.

CHAPTER FIFTEEN

Kory hurt so much she could barely breathe. Pent-up emotions weighed on her muscles and bones, craving release. She tensed against the onslaught, even as she straddled Will's legs and settled on his lap, knowing she'd face more emotion this way. But facing it was the only way through it.

When she looked at him, her heart torqued, and she had one thought. *Annihilate him. Make him feel your torment.* By the look of his heavy-lidded eyes when she rocked against him, he was halfway there.

How dare he add to her confusion and pain? Who gave him permission to become sympathetic, understanding, more than… whatever he'd been these last two months? She covered his mouth with hers and slid her palms to either side of his throat. On an inhale, she buried blunt fingernails into the back of his neck and squeezed.

Will groaned and arched beneath her, pressing the hard heat concealed by his boxers into the soft wet chasm between her legs, grabbing her none-too-nicely around the curves of her waist in the process. And it was glorious. Somehow the unrelenting pressure of his hands lessened the pressure in her chest, and she writhed on a wave of powerful, strange pleasure, grinding against him, kissing him mercilessly, until she had no choice but to release his mouth and gasp for air.

His hands lightened around her waist as he sat still beneath her, eyes wide, lips parted. She wondered if he was as stunned as she was. She wondered if he craved more. She wondered how far she should push this. And then it didn't matter, because the pressure returned to her chest, begging for release, demanding action without premeditation.

She gripped his chin and yanked his mouth to hers, willing him to inflict the same exquisite torture, to ease the pressure within, but his hands stayed soft as their lips.

Kory squirmed, eliciting another groan from deep inside his chest. She swallowed it along with her own. If she couldn't find lasting relief, neither would he. She dragged her mouth to his ear to tell him so. Instead, she played with the silky lobe between her lips, licking it, pulling it with her teeth until the pressure demanded more, and she bit him, hard enough to make him dig his fingers into her sides again as he rammed his erection into her core.

Yes, she almost screamed, but her lips stopped the word, permitting only a whimper, as they closed around his lobe, suckling the spot where she bit.

Will's panting echoed in her ear as his hands strangled her waist, crushing her hips. As magnificent as it was, Kory wasn't satisfied. She wanted more, needed more. Pressing her breasts to his bare chest, she abraded them over the spattering of hair, her nipples tightening until they throbbed. Her whimpers turned to moans, releasing some of the pressure.

In a flash of movement, Will had her by the wrists, pulling her body back, yanking her hands behind her waist. Shocked and breathless, she opened her eyes to his wicked smile as he admired her upper body arching toward him. Her chest quivered with every labored breath.

He gripped her wrists in one hand, and though she was strong enough to fight the position, she lost all desire to the minute his free hand roamed her body, stroking her, tickling her, making her close her eyes in an attempt to savor every sensation. She hated him. No, that wasn't right. She loved him. No, that wasn't right, either. Was it? The garbled thoughts stalled as the pleasure mounted.

An unexpected pinch to her nipple made her yelp, and heat flushed her body from head to toe. She opened her eyes as he dropped his head, soothing her burning breast with his tongue. How much more could she take?

Will's mouth dragged over her chest to her collarbone, to her jaw, distracting her enough that his fingers between her legs were a delicious surprise.

"Yes," she managed. *Just like this.*

And then he was hot and hard at her entrance.

Rising onto her knees, Kory granted him permission to enter, expecting him to release her wrists. Instead, he returned to his two-handed grip, pulling on her arms as he pushed inside. The stretch across her chest, mirrored the stretch between her legs, and the pressure consumed her, building with every collision of their hips, until she was moaning, battling his hands around her wrists, craning her mouth to his. Wanting it to stop. Wanting it never to end. More pressure. Deeper pressure. Making it harder to breath.

She broke the kiss, scraped her cheek over his, down his neck to his shoulder, where she rested her forehead, struggling for air while the frantic rhythm of their bottom halves guaranteed she'd stay breathless. So. Much. Pressure. In her chest. At her wrists. Between her legs.

Mouth open, tongue swirling over the soft, salty skin at the crook of his neck, Kory felt orgasm stir in her belly. *Just a little more*, she thought, as she rose up, rammed down and bit into his flesh without mercy.

• • •

Will roared as pain and pleasure ripped through him. The pulsing in his penis matched the pulsing in his neck, and his eyes rocketed open in shock.

She bit him, and he came. What the hell was that?

Releasing her wrists, he dropped his head to the back of the couch and stared at the ceiling while she collapsed onto him, her cheek pressing against the scene of her assault. Physically and emotionally exhausted, and battling the extra weight against his chest, Will struggled to breathe, struggled to make sense.

They'd had sex before, but not like this. Hell, he'd *never* had sex like this. Maybe he should apologize. The ache in his shoulder made him wince. But what did he have to apologize for? Holding her hands behind her back? She bit him. Twice.

As if she read his mind, she opened her mouth over the wound and bathed him in gentle kisses. He squeezed his eyes shut, holding all sorts of emotions in, not to mention three little words that would break his promise to not stand in her way.

Stay with me.

How could he let her leave after that? Whatever that was? How could he ever find it with anyone else? He didn't even know it was something he wanted. And now it was something he needed.

Wrapping his arms around her shoulders, he held her close, breathed her in, memorized the way her body molded to his, and she melted, going limp in his arms.

Stay with me.

He shook his head, frustrated beyond belief. Weeks ago he told her he wanted her, anytime, anywhere. Tonight, he offered her a job scenario that was his best possible shot at keeping her here. And then, he let her ravage him, use him, rip his heart out until he was just a shell. She had to know where he stood. He'd made it loud and clear.

It was her turn.

She pushed away from him, a small smile lifting her lips, and then she traced the sore spot on his shoulder. "I'm sorry," she whispered.

"I'm not," he said, even as the scrape of her nail made him wince. "It's something to remember you by."

She looked at him, blinked, and then blinked again. "Will, I..."

He waited. He hoped.

After what seemed like forever, she looked away, crossing arms over her breasts, and inch-by-inch he lost his connection with her, until she was gathering clothes from the floor.

"I have to go," she said. "Thanks."

He scoffed, mostly to hide the hurt that had nothing to do with the bite mark at the base of his neck. "For what?"

"For being so understanding." She didn't look at him. She slipped into her shoes and walked away.

As he watched her go, he felt a lot of things. Understanding wasn't one of them.

"You're making a mistake," he finally said.

But the door had long since closed.

• • •

Kory wasn't sure she could think straight enough to stay on the right side of the road, but she had to try. She had to get away.

So what if she was running? It didn't mean she was a coward. She was a self-preservationist. She couldn't stay and bask in the afterglow of something she didn't understand, something she might not ever have again.

Will, I wish we could make this work. Her brain finally finished the sentence her mouth refused to say. It would have been a waste of breath anyway. There wasn't a reasonable way to make it work, but Will would disagree. He thought it was reasonable for her to stay in Harmony Falls. She laughed...until she cried.

Under different circumstances maybe it would be reasonable.

Kory imagined the happy, stress-free life of being an underachiever, picked by Will Mitchell to warm his bed, keep his house, and raise his kids. The tears blurred her vision, and she willed them away. She wasn't cut out to be that woman.

The real kicker was Will wasn't asking her to be. He offered her jobs. He offered himself. All he asked for in return was whatever she was willing to give. And he took it all, including the darkness she never knew was there.

Her head hurt. Her heart hurt. So she rolled the windows down and drowned out thoughts with the roar of the wind. When she finally pulled into the driveway and glanced into the rearview mirror, she realized she looked every bit as awful as she felt. Worse? Her mother was waiting on the porch, rocking in the chair closest to the door, knitting piled in her lap. Kory glanced at the time on her phone. Aunt Jeanie had dropped her off an hour before the usual time.

"Is everything okay?" Kory asked as she pushed out of the truck.

Mom nodded, taking her in as she stepped onto the porch, no doubt noting her disheveled appearance. "Everything is fine with your father," she said. "But he was worried about you and thought I should come home early." She offered a pointed gaze, the kind that only a mother could give, the kind that said she knew there was something to worry about.

"I'm fine," Kory said, shrugging and pushing past her into the house. If she lingered and allowed a longer conversation, the truth would come out. Not the whole truth, but enough to validate her mother's worry.

"Where were you?" The screen door clanged behind her.

"Resigning."

"At Will's house?"

Kory swallowed and nodded as she bent to pet the dogs, knowing the less she said the better.

Mom was quiet for a long time. "How'd he take it?"

It seemed completely inappropriate to say he took it hard. "We'll all be a lot better off when I'm back in Chicago," she mumbled, because she needed it to be true.

"Well, your father's not so sure. He's worried you're leaving in a rush because of what you learned."

Maybe. But not because she couldn't handle what she learned, because it put things into perspective. Didn't it?

She straightened, rolled her shoulders back and attempted to breathe, but the vice around her chest returned, and she knew relief wouldn't come easy—maybe not at all, especially not without Will. *Or distance*, the practical part of her brain rebutted. *You never had trouble like this in Chicago.*

Boosted by her final thought, Kory spun around and hugged her mother. "I'm good. I promise. I'm just tired. I'll head up to bed, get some rest and talk to Dad in the morning."

Things always looked better in the light of day.

CHAPTER SIXTEEN

Will pulled open the glass door to his office building, feeling like a Mack truck ran over him in his sleep. He hoped to God Kory felt the same. She deserved to share in the misery she caused him. But a second later, he changed his mind. He wouldn't wish walking death on anyone.

"Good morning, boss." Georgiana smiled at him overtop her laptop screen.

He wasn't about to tell her just how lousy his morning was. He figured she'd catch on soon enough. "Morning," he said, snatching the daily paper off the corner of her desk. "Do you still have the list of places we advertised for a nursing home medical director?"

She blinked up at him. "I do."

"Re-run the ads immediately." He greeted her shocked expression with a crisp nod and strode into his office, determined to let work overtake him.

By noon, he was tired of everything. In what now passed through his life as good fortune, Lance agreed to play interim nursing home medical director until they found a replacement for Kory, but now that the home was full, Will had to pay the opportunist even more money than before.

Back in the red, but what choice did he have? People needed jobs, and his mother was still waiting in the wings with her "for sale" sign.

Will needed a break. He glanced at the clock on the wall. His lunch hour was to consist of a meeting about Justin's mayoral campaign, but he didn't want to deal with his family now.

He bolted.

Leaving the building and bypassing his car in the lot, Will walked the length of sidewalk parallel to the offices, and then turned right toward town. Fresh air. Sunshine. He walked at a brisk pace around the block. Maybe then he could settle and get back to business as usual.

One block turned into two.

Nodding and smiling at people who passed, Will felt like a fraud. He wasn't in any mood to be friendly. The fresh air and sunshine that dragged him outside with the promise of new perspective simply made him more miserable. It was too hot for a walk in a suit. But he kept going, because turning around and resigning himself to business as usual would mean facing the truth. Kory was leaving in a week, and the nursing home would likely fail without her. He wasn't going to fare much better, and there was nothing he could do.

The farther he walked, the hotter he got until he was uncomfortable enough to look for a break from the sun. Standing on the corner of Sixth and Main streets, his choices were few: the post office, the credit union or the pub.

We've got a winner, Will thought as he walked into the air-conditioned chill. Taking the nearest stool, he couldn't remember the last time he'd sidled up to a bar in the middle of the day. In his current mental state, it seemed ridiculously appropriate.

"Hey, Willy. This is a treat. What can I get you?" Dison Nabor tossed a white towel over his broad shoulder and reached across the bar for a handshake.

"A minute to think," Will said. A drink sounded awfully good, but which drink? A beer wasn't going to cut it.

"You got it. Flag me down when you're ready."

Alone with his thoughts—again—Will stared at the bottles gleaming on the glass shelves. They held every color of the rainbow. He wondered how many bottles he could sample before he keeled over. Not that he would ever try.

His pants pocket vibrated. Probably his mother. Again. He could imagine her pacing the floor of his office, wondering where he'd run off to.

Dison walked toward him, a tumbler of piss-yellow liquid in hand. "Try this." He set it in front of Will, and the liquid sloshed from the glass.

"What is it?" he asked, leaning in for whiff, holding his tie in place with the palm of his hand.

Dison laughed. "Fresh squeezed lemonade. Made it myself."

Will blinked up at him. "No, seriously. What is it?"

"I am serious. Thought you might like to start light since you're looking pretty heavy. You know if you do it in reverse, you're asking for trouble."

Will shook his head and lifted the glass. *Lemonade. You've got to be kidding.* But he didn't want to be rude.

When the bell above the door chimed, Will didn't turn around.

When Dison called out, "Two Mitchells in one day," Will didn't have a choice.

He turned to see Justin at the same time Justin's palm smacked against Will's back.

"How's it going, Dison?" Justin asked, sliding onto the stool beside Will.

"Can't complain. How 'bout you?"

"Newly married, remember? I can't complain either."

Dison's laugh echoed through the mostly empty bar, somehow managing to make Will feel worse.

"Why are you here?" Will asked, his voice low and directed at Justin. "Aren't you supposed to be in a campaign meeting with Mother?"

"I bailed. Alice had an emergency at the theatre." By the look of Justin's ridiculous smile the emergency involved little clothing.

That disgusted Will even more. "How does the candidate skip his own campaign meeting?"

"By setting his priorities. Happy wife. Happy life." Justin laughed.

Will shook his head. He did not want to be a prick about his brother's happiness, but in the face of his misery, it seemed cruel. "Seriously, Justin. Why are you here?"

"Well, I have people, and my people saw you walking into a bar in the middle of the day. They were concerned. I thought I should check on you."

Will couldn't begin to name Justin's people. This whole damn town would be on the list. So he shrugged, sighed and looked up at the bottles again. "I'm trying to figure out what to drink, something that will either give me enough balls to get on with things, or something that will knock me out cold so I don't have to deal with anything."

"Difficult decision," Justin said.

Out of the corner of his eye, Will saw his brother hold up two fingers, and in a blink, two beers were sliding toward them.

"Start slow," Justin said. "That way you can always change your mind."

"I got similar advice from the keeper." Will lifted the mug in a salute to Dison.

"Smart man," Justin said.

They drank in silence.

Four swigs in, Will set down his mug and angled his body toward Justin. "What will you do when Alice leaves you?"

Justin crossed arms over the bar and stared at Will. "Do you know something I don't know?"

"No, but one way or another, she's going to. Either she'll walk away, or they'll wheel her away in a casket."

"Jesus," Justin said, throwing back his beer for a good long drink. "I see you haven't made any progress in your mood since the wedding."

"What? I'm being practical."

"You're being miserable. And let me tell you, that's not going to help whatever has you miserable in the first place."

"Yeah? What will?"

Justin drank again. "Enjoying life while you can. Knowing when you've got it good. Can it be rough? Absolutely. Can it be wonderful? It can. Beyond your wildest dreams, man, but you've gotta take risks to get there."

"I don't even recognize you, man," Will said noticing the evaporating foam at the top of his beer. "What happened to the guy who touted familial duty before personal desire?" Will looked up. "By the way, you missed a button." He pointed to the third button on Justin's dress shirt, which was hidden behind his tie, but from Will's vantage point, it was obviously missing its hole.

Justin fiddled with the fastenings, righting the wrong, and then smoothing his tie back into place. He wore a smile the entire time. Will wanted to feel that carefree.

"That guy learned that there's more to life than pleasing powerful people who were never really going to have his back." Justin leaned closer, glancing at the other end of the bar where Dison chatted with a waitress. "Our mother could be included on that list. Trying to please her and striving for her stark approval led me places I never wanted to be. I didn't want a lifetime of that. I wanted more. Alice showed me more. And whether I have it for a lifetime, a decade, or a year doesn't matter, because in the end I had it, and it's proof I'm worth more than my last name and business acumen."

Kory showed Will more, too, and that's why her leaving hurt. Knowing he was more than his last name and business successes wasn't much of a consolation prize. "Maybe I'm more like Mother than you are. Maybe I'm destined for a cold life."

"Our mother isn't naturally happy, but she's not miserable by circumstance, either. She told me once there was no greater show of love to Dad than seeing his dreams through to fruition. She's not running this business and boosting this town for the personal power and accolades. She's doing this for him, because she loves him, because every time she walks into a meeting and sits at the head of the table, where he would've sat, she feels close to him. Say what you want about her warped lack of affection for us, but our mother loves our father as much, if not more, today than she did the day she married him. She just doesn't want to live a single day without him at the forefront of her mind, otherwise she would've dumped this business off on us completely and totally the minute we were old enough to run it."

Will sipped his beer, letting Justin's words ruminate. So what did that mean for Will?

"You know the sad truth? You and I are probably replaceable," Justin continued. "She could hire some other poor souls like she did after Dad died and we were too young to work. She could easily tell hired hands what to do. Mark, however, has job security, because nobody in his right mind would live with that woman and take care of her twenty-four hours a day."

Sad as it was, they laughed. The levity broke up some of the heaviness tightening Will's chest. Knowing he was replaceable probably should've upset him more than it did, but instead there was an odd sense of freedom that came with Justin's revelation. All these years, Will had felt somewhat trapped by his birthright, like the decision to take over the daily operations of Mitchell Company, Inc. wasn't his to make. Instead, he simply accepted it as his destiny, like Kory accepted Chicago as hers. Maybe they were both wrong. Maybe they had choices neither one of them was willing to make.

Will didn't know if that made him feel better or worse.

"Fill 'er up," Will called to Dison, pointing to the lemonade glass.

Until he figured something out, he wasn't going anywhere.

• • •

Kory rounded on patients slower than usual. After last night with Will, she was emotionally, mentally, and physically spent, which meant she was too raw and worn for her usual manic pace. Whatever happened between them had messed her up more than she wanted to admit. Even the bright light of day didn't take away the restlessness that lingered.

As she wandered the halls, moving in and out of rooms, she realized something else. Her days here were numbered. She suddenly and acutely found it bittersweet.

The red light glowed over Mrs. Ryan's door, signaling the need for an aide or nurse. In Chicago, Kory would've walked on by, but two months in Harmony Falls and ignoring a person in need simply because responding wasn't in her job description seemed inhumane.

"What can I do for you, Mrs. Ryan?" Kory asked as she stepped inside the room.

"Oh, hello, Dr. Flemming. It's time for my cream. Have you seen Judy? She rubs my feet before lunch every day."

Kory smiled. Foot massages were definitely not part of her job description in Chicago. Touching a patient outside a physical exam was a waste of precious time when forty other patients remained, which was a shame. Little things like this helped a doctor get to know her patients better.

She picked up the tube on the nightstand beside Mrs. Ryan's bed. "Is this what Judy uses?"

Mrs. Ryan nodded. "Yes, but surely you have better things to do."

"Absolutely not. In fact, I've been meaning to stop by and visit so I can hear all about Jacob."

While Kory rubbed Mrs. Ryan's feet, she caught up on Jacob Ryan's naval exploits. The more Mrs. Ryan talked about her grandson, the more she relaxed, and by the time Kory left the room, the woman who had struggled to get comfortable since the day she was admitted to Harmony Elder Care was asleep with a smile on her face.

Satisfaction warmed the back of Kory's neck, distracting her from other melancholy thoughts. She absentmindedly scratched the spot. An oddball professor back in med school had talked about healing with the head, hands, and heart, but she'd deemed his lectures as mostly noise. Kory preferred molecular and cellular coursework. Besides, all too quickly she'd learned care like Dr. Carmen espoused was a luxury she couldn't afford in Chicago, where the rehab center's business model dictated each doctor see an obscene amount of patients each day. There wasn't time for conversation with her patients. Walking the clean but dingy halls of Harmony Elder Care, she couldn't suppress the effervescence in her chest, because—surprise, surprise—care like that was possible here. Maybe she would find Dr. Carmen's email address and drop him a line, telling him she finally appreciated what he meant.

Kory stuck her head into the next room. "Morning, Mr. Weinstein." He was propped into a sitting position, but lilting to one side. She righted him and smoothed his covers. "How are you feeling today?"

As she went through the mundane motions, the satisfying warmth she felt lingered. She was a better doctor for her time here, wasn't she? A different doctor, that was for sure. Maybe she couldn't admit it until now, but she'd sensed it the day Mr. Martin died—even then, she was changing.

A full cup of applesauce sat on the tray hovering above Mr. Weinstein's bed. He'd been having trouble swallowing since a mild stroke compounded his already lengthy list of ailments. "Has anyone been in to help you with this?" she asked, gesturing to the applesauce.

He shook his head, gaze glued to *Law and Order* on the suspended television at the foot of his bed.

Kory glanced over her shoulder at the empty hallway. Someone would be around soon enough; there was a queue order to these things. But she was here now. Why not? Again, she recognized she wouldn't have the chance to be this close to patients in Chicago. The sadness returned.

"May I?" she asked, lifting the cup and a spoon.

He looked at her and smiled. "It'd sure be nice."

She smiled, too.

In medical school, everyone claimed to be there because they wanted to help people, but not Kory. She became a doctor for the rigorous academic challenge. Feeding Mr. Weinstein his applesauce, listening to his heartfelt thank you's after every bite, she realized while she may have become a doctor for the mental challenge, she was going to stay a doctor for the difference she made in people's lives, especially people like her father.

• • •

At three-thirty, a half hour before Kory intended to head home for an early dinner with her mother, Lance Palmer walked into her office, wearing full cycling gear.

"I had some down time, so I thought I'd stop by." He freed his head from the red, white and blue helmet and plopped in an empty chair on the opposite side of her desk.

She'd never liked him. He was an arrogant underachiever in her opinion, and whatever medical school stooped so low as to give him a degree needed to be closed.

"Do we have an appointment?" she asked, trying not to snicker at his ridiculous outfit.

"No." He shrugged. "But it's my day off, and I just accepted the interim medical directorship, starting the day you leave. I figured it'd be a good time to talk about what's been going on since I left. Mitchell seems to think this place can be lucrative based on what he's seen from you."

Lucrative? Hardly. And she couldn't imagine Will being naïve enough to think so, either. "This place can make a difference in people's lives, whether they're here as a patient or they're the loved one of a patient, but that's not always going to translate into a profit."

"Yeah. I was afraid of that." He sucked something out of his top teeth. "Nothing's changed, has it? Except you got some new beds. Nice. Oh, and my new contract has an extra zero." He laughed.

His flippant response smacked Kory across the face so hard she swayed back in her chair. This was the jackass who would be overseeing her father's recovery.

Her kneejerk reaction was to confront Will, ask him what he was thinking, but then sensibility overcame her. She knew what he was thinking. She was leaving, leaving him in a lurch, and Lance was the best he could do on such short notice.

You could stay. Her mother's voice echoed in Kory's head, and it remained even as she rushed Lance out and gathered her things. The louder the words grew, the more frustrated she became. She couldn't stay, just like that. People were counting on her. Her leave of absence from the rehab center impacted everyone else on the call schedule, and she'd verbally committed to a job that would need to be filled soon.

Still, Lance prattled on, and Kory squirmed under the weight of guilt that came along with leaving these people, people she cared about, with someone as uncaring as him. When he finally left, she rushed down the hall toward her father's room, acutely aware that these people were counting on her, too.

The pressure in her head fuzzed her vision. She'd thought she'd made her choice already. Chicago. Hands down. But as her pace quickened, she realized she was still stuck between a life of premeditation and this life of chance.

It was time to really choose.

CHAPTER SEVENTEEN

When Will returned to his office, his mother was waiting for him.

"Where have you been?" she asked, sounding every bit as annoyed as he expected her to be.

"Justin and I had a few drinks." And thankfully the sense of freedom lingered.

"In the middle of the day?" Her eyes were bulging.

"Yes, Mother, in the middle of the day. I have a lot on my mind. Kory gave her notice, and I've re-hired Lance."

His mother rolled her eyes. "Now, will you listen to me and sell that thing? It's nothing but a headache."

Will sat at his desk. "That *thing* is called home to forty-five people."

Mother wrinkled her nose and looked away.

"What do you have against Harmony Elder Care?" he asked. "I get the sense it's about more than profit margins."

She folded her hands in her lap and adjusted in her seat, refusing to look at him.

"Was Dad ever there?" Will couldn't remember every detail about his father's battle with cancer, probably because he blocked much of it out.

"Of course not." She scoffed. "I would've never disrespected him or our marriage by letting him waste away in there."

"Nobody's wasting away in there." Not under Kory's watch. Will pushed away the melancholy thought.

Mother huffed. "That's what your generation tells itself so you can go on with your lives without the burden of taking care of your parents."

"What are you talking about? Mark takes damn good care of you."

"And what if something happens to Mark?" She looked at Will, her wrinkled lips trembling. "You and Justin will lock me away."

Will's jaw dropped. "Wow. Your opinion of us is high."

Her silence contributed to the sinking in Will's gut. His mother really could be a coldhearted woman.

"So let me get this straight," he said." You want to sell that home because you're afraid of it."

"Don't be stupid." She looked away again. But it wasn't enough of a shield for him to miss the single tear, streaming down her cheek.

Will stood and rounded the desk. When he reached her side, he bent to pull her into a hug. "Nobody's going to put you anywhere you don't want to be."

She squirmed in his arms, and her inability to accept his comfort was even sadder than her fear. He stood and reclaimed his seat.

It was always going to be this way, wasn't it? Her thinking the worst of life and people in general. Her picking at him until he was making decisions solely with an aim to please.

Justin's words echoed: *Trying to please her and striving for her stark approval led me places I never wanted to be.*

Me, too, Will thought. And he definitely wanted a life filled with more than that.

• • •

By the time she reached her father's room, Kory's mother was gone, off to run errands in town like she did every Monday afternoon: the post office, the library, and the dollar store. Kory smiled, because the trip meant a fresh batch of hard candy on the kitchen counter tonight. But her smile faded when she realized she'd be getting her favorite candy through the mail this time next week.

"Hey, Dad," Kory said.

He smiled, and some of the tension she'd been holding in her shoulders went away. The half-smile that used to make her pity him was now a reminder of how far he'd come.

"How are you feeling today?" She moved in, grabbing his hands to test his grip strength.

He pulled his strong hand away. "Pull up a chair."

She lifted her brows. Normally, she thrilled at anything he said, but she was wary today. After her run in with her mother last night, Kory was certain her father was about to treat her to his first post-stroke lecture.

"I'm fine," she said, hoping to cut him off at the parental pass.

"Sit down," he said, so clearly she couldn't refuse.

When Kory perched on the edge of a bedside chair, he grabbed her hand again and squeezed. "I am proud of you."

"I know." She'd heard it so many times it sort of lost its impact.

"I love you."

"I love you, too." A routine exchange, as well, until she remembered the time immediately surrounding his stroke, when she wasn't sure she'd hear him say anything ever again.

Her heart fluttered against her ribs as she watched his lips twitch in preparation for more words.

"I do not have any regrets. Any," he said, squeezing her hand.

She nodded, fighting tears. "I know. It was a long time ago, and I don't hold any of it against either of you."

"No. You are not hearing me." He winced at the failing clarity of his words, and then he took a breath. "I am glad you are here, of course. But I am glad I am here. I would not change a thing."

He couldn't be talking about the hospital bed or the nursing home. Surely he'd like to get the heck out of here. "You're glad you're in Harmony Falls?" she asked.

He squeezed her hand again. "Everything I love is here." He tried to level her with his raised-brow-dad eye, and the lopsided attempt was endearing. He was clearly very tired, and she needed to let him rest.

It was Kory's turn to squeeze him. "That's good to know, Dad," she said, as she leaned forward, placing a kiss on his cheek.

"Love matters most," he whispered in her ear.

Kory flung an arm across him and rested her head on his chest. "Yep," she said, halting the word when it wavered with tears.

It was true. People didn't know how much they had until they almost lost it.

She lay there like that, listening to her father's heartbeat, so damn thankful that he was here and she was here...

"You could stay," said a voice from behind Kory.

She lifted her head from her father's chest.

"I'd like you to stay."

She faced the teary-eyed woman gripping shopping bags, standing in the doorway.

"Your father and I would like you to stay."

Dad squeezed Kory's arm.

"But you have to do what you want to do," Mom said, crossing the room and placing her bags on the dormant radiator. "Thank you for putting your life on hold for us. Having you here has been a tremendous comfort." She wrapped her arms around Kory, creating an awkward family hug. "And we just want you to know you're always welcome here."

Dad echoed Mom's sentiments.

Stuck between them, Kory stared into space. She'd waited a long time to hear those words, so long that she expected them to pack more of a punch. Maybe they didn't because they were just words she'd put too much emphasis on. Maybe they didn't matter now, because her heart always knew what her head had been too busy overanalyzing to see. Here, there, anywhere, her parents wanted her to be happy—no matter what it took.

What would it take?

For the first time in her life, Kory wasn't sure.

CHAPTER EIGHTEEN

Flipping a pen to his desk, Will cranked up the volume on his stereo, pressed his back to the chair, and closed his eyes, wishing away his obligations. He'd spent too much time at the bar with Justin and too much time trying to make sense of his meeting with his mother. As a result, he was going to have to work later than he'd planned, which sucked, because he didn't want to be here.

What if he could make it all go away? *Everything except Kory.*

Chicago. He yawned as the word floated in his head. He could see Kory there, rushing down shiny sterile halls, barking out commands. His chest squeezed, but he pushed through the discomfort and the next thing he knew, he was imagining himself there, too. He had enough education and experience to find employment outside Harmony Falls. He had enough money to start another business, too. And like Justin said, they were *replaceable.*

Chicago? He sat up, smacking his palms to the desk. What the hell was wrong with him? Why was he even entertaining such a thing? It didn't make sense. Why would he give up everything he'd accomplished here to take a chance there? Unless…Kory meant more.

It's about sacrifice and love so deep you give up what you want for the life and love of someone else. Her words repeated in his head, until he couldn't ignore the truth any longer.

He loved her. As clear as the blue sky bathing his office in unwanted sunshine, the thought roared through his head. Of course he loved her. Why else would he make concession after concession? Risk professional and personal sanity? And why wouldn't he? He'd never given more of himself to anyone, yet he'd never felt more whole than when he was giving everything he had to her. Kory challenged him, humbled him, and respected him, and he wanted to do the same for her.

Imagine what we'd be capable of if we banded together, she'd said back at the start of all this. They'd had the answer all along, and for all their combined smarts, they'd both been too dumb to see it.

He laughed like the sleep deprived, lunatic he was. The man who swore he didn't want a female in his life other than his dog, not only wanted Kory Flemming, he needed her. Thinking back to the way Kory bolted from his house, he had a hunch she knew it too.

Dropping his face to his hands, he sighed. All these years spent bad-mouthing—relationships should've protected him from love, but they didn't, and it sucked, because loving her didn't magically solve anything. It only changed the intensity with which he wanted her.

He lifted his head, looking around his empty office, feeling restless beyond anything he'd ever known. He had to find her. Tell her. Make her admit she loved him too. It might not change her departure date, but at least when she left he'd have one less regret.

"William, that parking lot needs repainting." He heard the voice before his mother blew into the office with Mark on her heels.

Yes, the yellow and white parking lines were faded, but Will could not have cared less. He had bigger concerns.

"I agree," he said, strolling toward her and placing a kiss on her cheek. "While I'm gone, why don't you and Mark make those arrangements?"

"Gone? What? I thought..."

He didn't hear the rest. He was already out the door and jogging down the hall.

• • •

Kory washed lettuce while her mother chopped vegetables. It was a routine and rhythm she'd come to enjoy. But tonight's ritual was solemn, with her mother keeping the conversation going.

"In your professional opinion, how long until he comes home?" Mom stopped chopping.

Kory shrugged. "Best case scenario? Another month. If he's motivated." She wouldn't be here to oversee the motivation. Her father's progress would partly depend on Lance. She grimaced and rubbed the heel of her hand at the ache in her breast.

"Well, he swung his legs over the side of the bed unassisted today." Mom smiled. "That must count for something."

"It does. It's awesome," Kory said, not feeling the magnitude of the word. She patted the romaine lettuce between paper towels and then looked up and out the kitchen window to the dogs racing across the yard. She couldn't turn her back on this place completely. "Maybe the job won't be quite ready for me when fellowship ends, and I can spend a couple weeks back here."

"Maybe," Mom said. The chopping quickened.

"That way I can keep a close eye on Dad, and push him if he's slacking."

"He would like that." She reached across the sink, bumping Kory in the process. "I'd like that, too."

Kory smiled, because it really was good to hear. "Then, I'll make it work." She hoped.

The start date for the assistant directorship was up in the air until the current director's promotion was approved. With any luck, the approval wouldn't come down until well after Kory finished fellowship. Then she could come home, see her parents, see Will…

"Are you going out tonight?" Mom asked.

It was a reasonable question. Kory had gone "out" most nights during the last several weeks, and she would be going out again tonight—just not to the usual place. She turned her head to hide her pained expression. There'd been no word from Will all day, not that she expected him to contact her after what happened between them last night. A clean break was probably better. Heck, he was moving on at a record pace, rehiring Lance less than twenty-four hours after she handed in her resignation. When she left the nursing home today, she actually thought staying in Harmony Falls was a possibility. Now, she wasn't so sure. She wished something definitive would happen to help her decide. Until then, she was moving forward with her plan to return to fellowship.

Taking a nice deep breath, Kory staved off disappointment. "Alice called earlier and asked me to help assemble programs. Since she's been volunteering at the nursing home for rec therapy, I figured it's the least I can do."

Mom nodded. "Sounds nice."

Another sound caught Kory's attention. Her phone vibrated against the countertop. She hopped toward it, mentally wishing for Will.

"Chicago," she murmured, spying the area code.

It could be anyone really. She'd made so many phone calls over the last two days, trying to shore up the life and opportunities she'd left behind. At the moment, she didn't feel like talking to any of them.

With the phone in hand and a constricting heart, she scrambled from the kitchen. "Hello?"

"Kory, it's Brooks Warren. Sorry it's taken me a couple days to return your call."

Speaking of the directorship…Kory sucked some air into her nose to calm the pounding in her chest. She probably shouldn't have sprinted to the living room. Sounding like a three-pack-a-day smoker wasn't the best way to impress her future boss.

"No problem, Dr. Warren," she said, managing to normalize her breathing. "You're a busy man." But sweat gathered beneath her hair on the back of her neck, making her squirm.

"That's an understatement." He inhaled nosily, and the sound had her holding her breath. "Listen, I realized the other day we haven't talked since you left, and then I left."

He left? Her jaw dropped. He couldn't leave. He was being promoted. She was going to fill the vacant spot that resulted from his promotion.

And suddenly, the rapid heartbeat and damp hairline took on a whole new meaning. It was as if her body had been trying to warn her something was amiss.

"I meant to call, before, during and after all hell broke loose, but starting a new job zaps all available energy," he continued the horrifying conversation. "My profuse apologies. Not just for the delay in calling you, but because the timing didn't work out for you. I talked to Lunderburn, and he told me about your leave of absence. I'm sorry about your dad, by the way. Anyhow, the good news is, you're young. One of the current directors is bound to leave before you're ready to retire." He actually chuckled, like it was no big deal. "You'll get your shot. In the meantime, you can go out there and spread your wings. Experience will only make you a better doctor."

Inch by inch, as his words and their meaning seeped in, Kory dropped to the couch. There was no job waiting for her in Chicago. She had the fellowship—a fellowship she pursued to position herself for this particular position—but she didn't have the job.

Now what?

When the call ended, Kory zombie-walked into the kitchen, where her mother put finishing touches on the dinner table.

"What?" Mom asked, dropping the silverware in a heap, coming to Kory's side. "What's wrong?"

"Everything." But then she took her deepest breath since the call ended, filling her lungs to capacity with the soft, warm scent of dinner rolls.

She looked at her mother's loving face. Losing that job didn't mean she lost this. And two months ago, she'd come close to real loss—her father. But he was here. Losing that job didn't mean she lost him, either. She gave her head an admonishing shake.

"What happened?"

As Kory relayed the conversation to her mother, losing the job hurt less and less, until she was breathing easier than she had in days. But why?

"I'm so sorry, baby." Wrapping an arm around her waist, Mom pulled her in.

Kory shrugged, overwhelmed by the unexpected relief. "Hey, the good news is, two weeks home after fellowship is totally doable now." She actually smiled.

While they ate, her mind raced. Why wasn't she more upset over the news? She'd never lost a position to someone else. That alone should've devastated her.

The screen door clanged.

"I brought dessert," said Aunt Jeanie, breezing into the kitchen with a strawberry pie in hand.

Mom stood and kissed her sister, taking the pie in the process. "Milt must be sad. You should've left it for him."

Aunt Jeanie winked at Kory. "He's on a diet." And then she pulled out a chair and sat. "One is plenty. I made two." She laughed.

Kory laughed, too. It was all so thoroughly confusing. She hadn't laughed with the people she loved in months. One phone call, which demolition-balled her future, and she was cackling? Crazy.

Mom and Aunt Jeanie stared at her.

"What?" Kory asked, wiping sputters of wet from her lips. "The idea of Uncle Milt on a diet is hilarious."

The sisters laughed and nodded in unison.

"It's good to see you happy," Mom said.

Was that what this was? Kory simply smiled.

Listening to the women talk as they ate dessert and cleaned up, the truth became clear. Life in Chicago was no longer planned out before her. With the end of fellowship came freedom. *Freedom.* Had she ever really felt the full capacity of that word? She could apply for jobs anywhere in the world, and she could come home whenever she liked, because her parents wanted her here…because she wanted to be here…because everyone she loved was here.

Including Will.

Her chest pinched. She needed to tell him.

CHAPTER NINETEEN

Will drove slowly, trying to get up enough courage to pull into the Flemming's driveway and say what needed to be said—in front of Kory's mother if need be. Because he was a grown ass man, not a coward.

Who knew three little words could reduce him to rubble? It would be over in a matter of seconds. Worst-case scenario she laughed in his face, which was nothing she hadn't done before. Best-case scenario, she said she loved him, too. And she would stay.

Okay, that last part was enough wishful thinking to drain his courage again. But here was the thing…if Chicago was where she wanted to be, then he would consider being there, too.

"Final pass," he growled as he rolled through the stop sign at the corner of Rural Route Ten and Baker Farm Road. If he didn't make it into the driveway and out of the car this time, he was going home.

The minute he turned onto her road and didn't see her father's pickup truck parked next to the white farmhouse, a thick dread consumed him. Her mother didn't drive, and her father wasn't able, so the only other person who would drive the truck was Kory. But where? With as much ground as he'd covered, they should've crossed paths.

He pushed out of the car and across the lawn until he was standing at the front door, knocking. It was the principle of the thing. If she wasn't here, she wasn't here, but at least he didn't chicken out.

The dogs howled, and he backed away.

Three steps off the porch, his phone rang. *Kory.* His heart slammed into his throat.

"Hello." He wasn't sure if he actually got the word out.

"Hi. Will, I need to see you."

Man, did that sound good. His smile triggered some relief. "I need to see you, too. I'm in your driveway. Where are you?"

"The theatre. I'm helping Alice."

He closed his eyes on a surge of disappointment. He did not want to have this conversation with his sister-in-law present. "When will you be home?"

She paused so long he could count his breaths. "Can you come here, Will? Please."

The sound of her voice alone could've brought him to his knees. "I'm on my way."

• • •

Kory hung up the phone and glared at Alice. "This is a crazy idea. I can't believe I let you talk me into this."

"This is perfect," Alice said, grinning and clapping like the queen of melodrama she was.

"He will never fall for it."

"Yes, he will. If he's half as messed up as Justin says he is, he won't be thinking straight for months. I can convince him to do anything."

Closing her eyes and shaking her head, Kory cursed her big mouth, wishing she had kept it shut when it came to what happened in the coat checkroom during Alice and Justin's reception. If she had, Alice wouldn't have been able to use the information to concoct this silly plan.

"I can't do this," Kory said. "It's stupid."

"You can, and you will." Alice grabbed her hand and pulled her towards the theatre's coat checkroom. "It's a brilliant idea if I say so myself."

"That's because it's your idea." Kory groaned and smacked her free hand to her forehead. "He's going to laugh at me."

"Laughter is good. Let him laugh, because as soon as you say what you want to say, your mouths will be too busy for words." She giggled.

Kory's stomach heaved. She should've met him at his house, but Alice insisted a moment like this required pizazz. *Pizazz*. Kory didn't do pizazz. "I'm going to be sick," she said.

"No, you're not. You're going to be happy," Alice said, opening the door and pushing Kory inside. "Sit in the corner and wait. As soon as he heads for this door, I'll leave. I promise. Then you can have the whole place to yourself." She winked.

"I am not having sex in your theatre."

"Your loss." She grinned, and then she blew Kory a kiss. "Good luck."

Kory pressed fingers to her lips as the door started to close. She was definitely going to be sick.

Alice's head reappeared. "Do you want a costume?"

"No," Kory yelled, releasing a few nervous laughs in between breaths.

The door clicked shut and Kory slumped into the armchair. This really was nuts. All she wanted to do was tell Will there'd been a change of plans after fellowship. She didn't have a job shored up in Chicago. She was free to do whatever she wanted to do. And loving him was on that list. Somehow things got all crazy, and she was now supposed to seduce him in a coat checkroom. Although after what she did to him on his couch, this was mundane.

The thought made her smile.

Fine, if she was going to be seducing him in a coat checkroom, she should probably look…seductive. Her stomach tumbled again. They didn't teach seduction in medical school. She glanced at the white oxford hanging loosely over denim capris. If she were Alice, she'd ditch it all and sprawl across the armchair naked. She was so not Alice. Instead, Kory unbuttoned the top three buttons of her shirt and leaned forward at the waist, propping her breasts into place. All the while her brain teased her, because she couldn't be this smart and not see how dumb she looked.

Standing with a huff, she tied the blouse at her waist, revealing plenty of skin, and tugged her jeans lower on her hips. That was as seductive as she would get.

And then she heard voices.

Her heart stopped as she held her breath. Was it Wren? Maybe her grandmother was feeling better and she decided to come after all. Kory's face heated with embarrassment. As much as she liked Wren, she wasn't sure she liked her enough to let her in on this sort of thing.

She pressed her ear to the door, and a familiar deep voice buckled her knees.

Shit. Shit. Shit. She looked around for an escape. Why did she let Alice talk her into this?

But it was too late. Kory closed her eyes, took a few deep breaths and backed herself into the corner. What was the worst that could happen? He'd laugh at her. Not like he hadn't done it before. Embarrassing images from high school flashed in her mind, but they'd come too far for her to give credence to them now.

Kory exhaled and flashed a nervous smile. Will Mitchell started something in a coat checkroom two months ago, and tonight, in this one, she was going to finish it.

• • •

Will rolled his eyes at his sister-in-law. "Why can't I just go up and talk to her for a minute?"

"I said I'll get her for you. Why are you being such a pill?" Alice huffed. "Besides, I need you to lift a heavy box off the top shelf in that room." She pointed across the lobby as she moved in the opposite direction. "Top shelf. About this big." She held out her hands, shoulder width apart. "Breakable stuff, so be careful. And take your time."

If he wasn't mistaken, she giggled. He turned around to call her on it, but she was gone, the only sign of her was the slowly closing door that led into the theatre.

Will shook his head. She was up to something. Maybe Kory was too. The more he thought about it, the more Kory had sounded funny on the phone. The question was, did she sound funny good or funny bad? He couldn't remember. He'd been content to hear her voice.

If he survived this night, it would be a miracle.

Inhaling, he pulled on the doorknob of the room Alice pointed to, and stepped inside.

"Surprise."

It was a soft unexpected sound, and he stepped back, more than surprised. Maybe even a little scared. He didn't often walk into rooms and find...

Kory perched on the arm of an overstuffed chair, smiling like she wasn't sure she should be smiling. The result was a cockeyed grin that socked him right in the groin.

"What's going on?" he asked, taking in the rest of her. A white oxford shirt knotted seductively at her waist and unbuttoned enough to show off perky boobs. Faded jeans slung low on her narrow hips and led to blessedly bare feet. Hell, he couldn't even remember why he was here. He was just so damn glad he was.

"Well..."—she stood, took a deep breath and wiggled those hips toward him, her blue jeans sliding lower—"...you started something in a coat room once, and I'd like to finish it."

The sultry words and movements were in direct contrast to her raised brows and her teeth worrying her bottom lip. It was an intoxicating combination. Will swallowed a groan, but a gruff noise still managed to escape.

She smirked at the noise, realization of the power she had over him written on her face. As if she could get any more beautiful... He groaned again as she slid her hands up his chest and over his shoulders, locking them behind his neck.

To think he'd spent the drive to town scared beyond reason to face her. *Her.* And here she was with her arms around his neck and her luscious lips smiling up at him, when twenty-four hours ago he thought he'd lost her forever.

Was he dreaming this? Was there something in that lemonade?

"I love you," he whispered, deciding to really test the limits of his good fortune.

Under the circumstances, his announcement was a little abrupt, so he wasn't surprised when she opened her mouth and released a squeal. The meaning of the squeal was indiscernible, but even if it was meant to be a negative noise, it was better than a slap across the face. And when she didn't step back, out of his reach, he took that as an even better sign. Now, if she'd just say something to put him out of his misery.

"I love you, too." Her face wrinkled. "But you beat me to it. I wanted to say it first."

Of course she did.

He wrapped her up in his arms and chuckled against her temple. "We're going to be battling like this for the rest of our lives, aren't we?"

"I hope so," she whispered. "Because honestly, I need you to call me out occasionally. For instance, remember when I said this was *nothing*?"

Will nodded. "I remember that night very well."

"Yeah, see, I was wrong. *Nothing* ended up being *something*, something really amazing."

"I tried to tell you that."

"Did you? I don't remember. Your mouth was kind of distracting."

He pulled back and cupped her face in his hands. Her lips glistened in the overhead lighting, drawing his mouth like a magnet. "So is yours," he said.

Kory stopped the kiss with her fingertips. "Wait. I have more to say." Eyes wide, lips straight. The playfulness had left her face.

His stomach bottomed out, like maybe the things she had to say wouldn't be things he wanted to hear, but he was holding her, looking her square in the eyes, and she loved him. How bad could it be? Whatever it was, he could deal.

"I lost the job in Chicago." Her eyes flashed downward, but then she looked up at him with a full-blown smile.

It confused the heck out of him. "I'm sorry?" The inflection of his voice mirrored his confusion.

"Don't be. I'm not. I mean, I was, but then I thought about what it really means." She played with his collar, her gaze flashing from his throat to his eyes. "It means I have some unexpected freedom after fellowship, and I can decide what comes next."

He hated to jump to conclusions. He'd never been that kind of guy. He'd also never wanted anything more than this, so it was probably reasonable he equated her unexpected freedom with them building a life together. Marriage didn't seem like such a bad deal, now...if it was what she wanted.

He'd give her anything.

Will's hands had a mind of their own, dropping to her shoulders, and then over her back, smoothing the bare skin of her midriff. He remembered the last time he grabbed her there, holding on for dear life, giving more of himself than he ever thought possible. A wicked heat spread over him, and he pulled her hips against him.

"Have you decided what comes next?" he asked, swirling his tongue around his dry mouth, eager for her to get to the point, so he could get to his.

"Well, first, let me say I believe in finishing what I start." She grinned as she unbuttoned his shirt.

"Thank God," he said, exhaling.

"I have to go to Chicago for the next month and finish my fellowship." Her mouth landed on his Adam's apple. "In the spirit of finishing what I started. It will be a busy month, and I won't have time to visit."

He had a busy month, too, which sucked, but he could handle the separation if afterwards they found a way to be together.

"I understand," Will said, his voice gruff beneath the pressure of her lips. "And then what?"

He reached around to the knotted cotton below her breasts, and worked to unfasten it, startling when she yanked his collar down, over his shoulder, and her tongue tipped the bruise she'd left the night before.

"And then I'm coming home. For good." She looked at him, her brows high on her head. "And when I do, Lance Palmer will not be welcome in my nursing home unless he's a patient. Understand?"

Will laughed, filled with an overpowering joy. This woman was made for him. She loved him. And she was coming home.

Any lingering bubbles of doubt popped, leaving him buoyant. He lifted her off the ground into a crushing hug. "I love you," he said, and then he said it again. Because he felt like it. Because he could. Because he never imagined it would be the wrong time or place to say those words again.

• • •

Kory pressed her mouth and nose against Will's neck and breathed him in as he held her off the ground. Normally, this wasn't a position she'd be comfortable with, but at the moment, she didn't care if he ever put her down.

Will Mitchell loved her, and she loved him. She almost laughed, because nobody who knew their history could've seen this coming. Maybe that's what made it so special. All the days and months and years her path was strong and straight in the absolute opposite direction of Will, but then life shook things up, shook her up, and put him square in her path. She could've been happy in Chicago, but she was so much happier here.

That was what her father was trying to tell her, wasn't it? Despite the altered course of his life, he wouldn't change a thing. Funny how, even though it was in a different context, history had a way of repeating itself.

"Let's get out of here," Will whispered as he lowered her to the ground.

Any other time, Kory would've followed him. But standing here, looking up at his smiling face, she couldn't imagine letting the opportunity go to waste. She scoffed as she tugged the shirttails from his pants and unfastened the lower buttons. Euphoria was one heck of an aphrodisiac.

"Didn't we just talk about the importance of finishing what we started?" she asked.

He tipped his head toward the door. "But Alice..."

"Won't come back. She promised to go and stay gone." Kory smoothed her palms over his warm belly, up to his chest.

Will closed his eyes and smiled. "You set me up, didn't you?"

She laughed. "You are a slow learner," she said, pushing the shirt from his shoulders, watching it slip from his arms. To think there was ever a day when she felt out of her league with Will Mitchell. "Lucky for you, I'm obscenely smart." She inched her face closer, bringing her lips almost to his. "And I don't mind tutoring a struggling man."

In a whoosh of motion, he lifted her again, this time depositing her onto the armchair amid mutual laughter.

"We'll see about that," he said, looming over her. "If I remember right, my I.Q. has a good ten points on yours."

"Will, Will, Will," she clucked, gripping him by the waistband. "Don't you know anything? It's not the size of your I.Q. that counts. It's the size of your…"

He cut her off with his mouth.

Laying beneath him, warmed by his body and an unmistakable inner glow, she realized life would be filled with countless choices… but never a better choice than this.

About the Author

Elley Arden is a born and bred Pennsylvanian who has lived as far west as Utah and as far north as Wisconsin. She drinks wine like it's water (a slight exaggeration), prefers a night at the ballpark to a night on the town, and believes almond English toffee is the key to happiness. Elley writes contemporary romances with flirt and flair for Crimson Romance. For a complete list of Elley's books, visit *www.elleyarden.com*.

More from This Author

(From *Crashing the Congressman's Wedding* by Elley Arden)

Alice shoved her feet into rhinestone-studded pumps, checked her teeth for smudges of red lipstick and dashed out the door onto the porch. She had exactly twenty minutes to get to church. Digging into her late mother's beaded clutch, Alice cursed her missing keys and walked as she rummaged, wishing a chat with the mail lady hadn't put her behind schedule.

Ruff. Mouse ran a zigzag pattern across the front yard, brushing filthy fur against her toile skirt.

"Stop it. You're dirty." Alice waved the dog away, but he brushed by again, causing her to stumble and step in a pile of ...

"Crap!" She threw her handbag to the ground and stared at the clump of brown on the tip of her shoe. "Are you serious?" She tossed her head back and roared at the cloudless sky. "You've got to be kidding me."

Stomping her way back to the porch, she kicked off the shoe and scraped the toe in the too-tall grass. Dog doo smashed between the rhinestones. Alice growled, dropped the shoe to the ground and limped into the house, heading straight for her only other pair of remotely matching heels ... character shoes. Wearing beige stage shoes wasn't the fashion statement she hoped to be making today, but she didn't have a choice. She was already late, and the only place to buy shoes in Harmony Falls was the thrift store, which was closed for the congressman's wedding.

These were the moments when Alice missed her mother most. She kissed fingertips and pressed them to Mama's face, smiling at

Alice from behind dusty glass. "Tough day, Mama. Wish you were here."

With a frown, Alice hastily fastened the shoes, leaving too much slack. At least the whole day hadn't been a bust. Shirley had delivered mail early on account of the wedding, and in her hand was a letter from the Arts Foundation. Alice's application was a finalist, which put her one step closer to opening an honest-to-God theatre in Harmony Falls. No more *The Sound of Music* in the park pavilion. No more *Peter Pan* in the church social hall. No more Poor Little Alice Cramer, the girl with impossible dreams.

She sighed and then smiled, determined not to let the bad parts of the day drown out the good.

Ten minutes remained, and Alice still had no idea where to find her keys. For all she knew, Mouse stole them again so he could chew on her lucky rabbit's foot. When she rolled her eyes, she noticed her brother's keys hanging on the hook by the door where he'd left them when he rode off with a group of deadbeat friends. Her nose crinkled. Charlie's car smelled like cigarettes and was littered with trash, but it would get her to the church faster than walking.

Snagging the metal off the hook, Alice tiptoed through the grass (careful not to step in anything questionable) and scooped her purse from the front yard before plopping into the driver's seat of Charlie's car.

"Ouch!" She dug a hand underneath yards of scratchy skirt and pulled out a tiara. The glistening crown was pretty. A bit odd, too. And it definitely wasn't hers. She tossed the headpiece into the backseat and shook her head. How Charlie managed to get any woman into this car willingly was beyond Alice. She kicked aside empty paper cups, shut the ashtray, rolled down the windows and pressed pedal to the floor all the way to church.

Making it with a few minutes to spare, Alice paused at the back of the sanctuary, smiling down the lily-lined aisle at the smoking hot man standing before the altar. His tuxedo was tailored, his shoulders were back and his hair was impeccably groomed. He'd worn the same lift to his blond bangs since high school. Back then, the fashionable hair blended with city-bought clothes to make him look even more privileged than he was. Now, almost fifteen years and two professional titles later, the flip of his bangs made her smile, because she recognized it for what it was—who he was—a predictable, responsible, creature of habit.

Alice sighed, smoothed a hand over the snug bodice of her dress and tried to remember a time when she didn't love Justin Mitchell.

He saw her then, and she dug deep into her theatrical bag of tricks to smile with a sincerity that would charm sight-challenged ladies in a theatre's back row. He bought it, smiled back, and Alice imagined the fine lines crinkling around his green eyes. The breath she tried to take stuck in her too-small throat, and she remembered she needed to walk, needed to move, needed to take her place. This wasn't the time for longing or regrets. This was a wedding.

The man she loved was getting married.

But he wasn't marrying her.

Alice released the misery with a shake of her head and then scanned the noisy crowd for friendly faces. Ken and Carole Flemming sat three pews from the altar, three pews too close to the fire, with an empty space between them where Kory should be. Today of all days, Alice missed her best friend, but resident doctors didn't get time off for non-family weddings—even if those weddings featured small-town royalty.

Sucking a mouthful of air, Alice took a step down the aisle. Although she preferred Mrs. Flemming's quiet smile to the rambunctious fawning of just about everyone else in town, for once in her life the attention that went along with a walk down the center aisle wasn't appealing. Alice chose relative anonymity in the back of the church instead.

She slid into the pew and studied the groomsmen, imagining her brother in the mix. Aside from Will and Mark Mitchell, Charlie knew Justin longest; he deserved to be up there, too. She closed her eyes and pictured Charlie cleaned up, with his bow tie tilted and his boutonniere hanging off his lapel. But when she opened her eyes, he wasn't there. Congressman Mitchell couldn't take the risk. Bonds of childhood friendship were no match for the potential embarrassment of having a drunk at the front of the church.

Alice's stomach clenched as she wondered if Charlie was sober today—wherever he was. If not, she prayed he stayed safe and out of too much trouble. She'd been praying for that a lot lately. And she'd keeping praying and hoping it wasn't too late, that Charlie wouldn't end up like their father.

The thoughts tugged acid into Alice's throat, and she held a hand to her mouth. Dropping her shoulders on a heavy exhale, her head followed. Too much emotion for one day. A loose piece of silver thread hung from the bottom of her skirt, and she felt tears that had nothing to do with the thread.

If it weren't for the false eyelashes and extra coats of mascara, she'd have allowed herself a good cry. Justin was getting married, and although she knew this day would come, the finality hit hard.

She sniffed, dabbed beneath her eyes with her knuckles and lifted her head, smile firmly in place. The church teemed with people who had every reason to celebrate. Congressman Justin Mitchell, chief financial officer of Mitchell Company, Inc., was making good on his late father's promise to bring life to this dying town. His congressional term set the stage for tax breaks and corporate-friendly zoning, and his arranged marriage would align the two most powerful families in the state. It didn't hurt that as a wedding present, the bride's uncle promised his new plastics plant to Harmony Falls.

So Alice loved Justin. Big deal. Who was she to stand in the way of progress?

Maisy Carmicheal twisted in her pew. "You look lovely, dear." She smiled at Alice and adjusted her cotton candy pillbox hat. For a beautician, the woman wouldn't know style if it stole her ugly hat and slapped her upside the head. "Wait until you see the bride. Perfection. My best updo ever."

"I'm sure." Alice held her eyes firmly in place despite the urge to let them roll down the aisle. Of course Morgan Parrish was perfect. Her father was the mayor. His power and money made certain she was skinny, educated, and flawless—everything Alice wasn't.

More tears burned the backs of Alice's eyes, but before a drop could fall, a flash of red passed on the Alice's left. Josie Parrish stopped beside Maisy's pew. "The combs aren't holding," she hissed. "Help me, Maisy. This is a disaster. I can't believe she lost that tiara. I told her that bachelorette party was a foolish idea."

Tiara? Hmmm. Alice watched the bride's mother grab Maisy around the wrist and pull her out of the sanctuary. *A tiara.* Like the one Alice sat on in the front seat of Charlie's car? *No.* Alice couldn't imagine Morgan ever stooping low enough to accept a ride from the likes of Charlie. And why would Charlie have been anywhere near Morgan's bachelorette party?

Alice shook her head. The tiara in Charlie's car couldn't be the same tiara Morgan was missing. Besides, after all the years of friendship, Charlie would never hurt Justin.

But a drunk Charlie did things a sober Charlie would never do.

Alice winced. Absolutely not. She refused to believe it. This was just an uncanny coincidence. And yet…how many tiaras were floating around Harmony Falls?

She looked at Justin. He held his hands waist high and alternated squeezing palms, first the right on top and then the left. From the back of the church, she couldn't see him clearly, but she bet he was chewing his bottom lip. He always chewed when he was worried. She couldn't shake the feeling that maybe he had something to chew about.

A few minutes later, Maisy returned to her pew. "Just a little hair snafu, but I worked my magic. The bride is officially breathtaking," she said, gloating loudly enough for several rows to hear.

Alice fidgeted, trying to push thoughts of missing tiaras out of her head. She scratched at her tight bodice, picking at a hard piece of plastic that ran up her side and dug into her right breast. When she did, her elbow bumped the man sitting next to her.

"You look pretty, Alice." The Mitchell's ancient gardener smiled and tipped his hat. "Just like Marilyn Monroe."

"That's sweet, Tubby. Thank you." Never mind that the dress was about as comfortable as a potato sack. She didn't remember it being so itchy when she wore it last year in *Hello, Dolly.* Then again, with no operating budget for her twice-a-year productions, the dress hadn't been dry-cleaned since.

Alice sighed again. Maybe borrowing a dress from the costume closet wasn't the best idea, but her alternatives weren't any better. Wear a frock from the thrift store or drop a bundle on a trip to the city and a dress she'd never wear again. In all honesty, this was hardly the occasion to splurge. She'd have worn black if she thought she could've gotten away with it.

Tubby started humming show tunes under his mint-scented breath, and Alice wondered if he recognized the dress. She slipped down in the pew, wishing she could hold her head up high, wanting just once to attend a Mitchell affair without sitting in the back with the outcasts. But Johnny Cramer made sure his daughter knew her place. Even though he died years before Mama, his words rang clear: "When they look at us, all they see is trash, baby. The sooner you realize it, the better off you'll be."

Yeah? Well, Alice realized it—and she was tired of waiting for the better-off part. All she needed was the grant money, and she'd have a real brick and mortar theatre. She'd know her place then, and everyone else would know her place, too.

Alice Catherine Cramer belonged in the spotlight, not in the audience. She deserved applause, not pity. And with that little pep talk, she smiled, fidgeted again and pressed her back to the uncomfortable pew.

A crinkled hand landed on her leg. "Maybe I'm the only one who thinks it, but that boy's making a mistake." Tubby shook his head. "A man should be happy on his wedding day, and he's not happy."

Alice blinked. Her mouth fell open, and she almost agreed, but before the words tumbled out, trumpets blasted through the church, and Molly Lunsford, cousin of the bride, tossed a handful of rose petals over the white runner near Alice's pew. She looked like a cherub with ringlet curls. The crowd oohed and aahed, and the child bowed. After another handful of petals hit the ground, the little girl sprinted down the aisle toward her papa, where he scooped her into his arms and planted a kiss to her cheek.

Sweet. Alice stole a glance at Justin. Despite the precious child and chuckles from the pews, he was somber, and his misery made her heart hurt. Before she could dwell too much on Justin's lack of happiness, creampuff bridesmaids strolled past, each one stuffier and stiffer than the next. Alice didn't know most of them. They were outsiders, Morgan's friends from a fancy law school in Connecticut, with poufy hair, chandelier earrings and bright pink lips. They looked like the cast of *Willy Wonka* threw up all over the stage.

And then Morgan appeared. The only thing missing was the choir of angels. She was five foot ten with hair of spun silk and a designer dress flown in from France. Whatever the Parrish family had paid for all those layers of lace, they paid too much, Alice thought, smoothing her hand-me-down dress over clenched thighs. She imagined all the overpriced clothes Morgan would buy with the Mitchell family money. What a waste.

The Justin Alice knew wasn't like that. He spent his money, drove new cars, and owned nice homes, but he gave a lot of his money away, and he looked best in blue jeans and a faded Penn State hat with the brim brushing his neck. Morgan wanted to change him, starting with the push to move to D.C. and the "for sale" sign in Justin's front yard. If the banshee got her way, Justin would turn into suit-and-tie-wearing Congressman Mitchell full-time and leave Harmony Falls for good.

As much as the thought depressed Alice, his complete transformation was for the best. When Plain Old Justin was around, Alice couldn't breathe. The lines blurred. He didn't seem so off limits wearing faded jeans and a crooked smile, and she didn't feel so unworthy. In those moments, dreams of being together spilled into her days, and she wasted time walking around a fool in unrequited love.

Thankfully, it'd been a long time since Alice had been stuck in the "I love Justin" rut. She was happy with the direction her life was headed. After today, she hoped the rut would be permanently patched. A girl could dream, couldn't she? Yes, she could. Even if those dreams weren't likely to come true.

A trumpet blast startled Alice as Morgan floated down the aisle with her nose in the air. Alice refused to fawn over a bratty bride, so she focused on the groom instead. His face lengthened and two shadows slashed his cheeks. There wasn't an ounce of joy in the man.

Smile, Justin. Although it would hurt Alice more to see him smile, even the smallest sign of happiness would set her free with the knowledge that at least one of them was getting what they wanted. The idea that he harbored second thoughts pushed her to the edge of the pew.

Smile, Justin. She willed her thoughts over the terrible trumpeting.

But Justin wilted further. There was no shine, no sparkle, no …tiara.

Alice gasped. What if the tiara in Charlie's car was Morgan's? What if they … ? She slapped a hand over her mouth. Charlie had been known to romance anything with the right parts, and Morgan's parts were in demand. If Charlie had been drunk, it was possible he made a move.

Oh, God. Alice bit the inside of her cheek. She'd been called a drama queen more times than she could count. Was she being overly dramatic now?

While the Parrish side of the wedding party beamed, the Mitchell side paled. Even Mark, the youngest and goofiest brother, looked worried. And why shouldn't he be? Everything was wrong. This wasn't a wedding march, this was a funeral dirge. The black cloud that appeared over Harmony Falls the day Justin's daddy died had grown into a full-blown storm with Justin directly in its path. And he didn't deserve to be. He was a good man who spent his days helping everybody else. Now it was time for somebody to help him.

The honorable thought carried Alice to her feet. She gulped a few mouthfuls of air, trying to gain courage. "Stop." The shaky command travelled a few pews.

Half the church looked at Alice instead of the bride.

"Can I talk to Justin?" Alice spoke louder this time, pushing out of the pew and into the aisle. "It'll only take a minute. I promise."

Alice hadn't heard so many gasps since she fell off the pavilion stage into the shrubs during opening night of *A Chorus Line*. But she kept her eyes on a gaping Justin, and blocked out the rest.

"Daddy, she's ruining my wedding."

Mayor Parrish stepped in front of his whining daughter and cut off Alice's view of the groom.

Alice stopped cold, watching the mayor move closer. "Justin, I… "

A couple hands wrapped around her upper arms, and Alice felt tugged from behind. "Let's go, little lady. No time for drama. This here ain't a thee-a-ter."

Alice didn't know whose hands were dragging her from the church. Frankly, she didn't care. Her character shoes caught on the runner as Mayor Parrish turned to console his daughter, and that was when Alice saw Justin, his mouth still hanging open.

"She's missing her tiara." Alice looked away from Justin and over the gaping crowd. "Charlie has it." Her voice cracked.

"Get out," Morgan screeched.

The next thing Alice knew, heavy doors shut in her face and Gilbert Hoover plopped her on a cement step. "Go home, little lady. Fix yourself some tea. It'll be all right. You'll see."

What did Gilbert know about all right? He pumped gas for a living. He lived in a doublewide. The pancake breakfast was his idea of gourmet "eats." This town was mad, and she was neck-deep in their insanity. Well, no more. It might be honorable to help a man who was making a terrible mistake, but from now on, Alice Cramer was only helping herself.

Justin could marry the banshee. Alice was going home. She lifted her skirt and stomped barefoot down the church steps.

"Where're your shoes?" Gilbert called.

It seemed her dignity wasn't the only thing Alice left lying in the aisle.

• • •

Justin stared at his beet-red bride-to-be as she cowered in her father's arms. Strands of inky silk slid from her hair combs and stuck to her wet cheeks. "What's going on?"

She burrowed deeper into her father's chest. "Alice is crazy."

Maybe. Charlie's little sister had done a lot of crazy things in her life, but standing up in church without good reason seemed extreme, even for a Cramer.

Between Morgan's sniffles, Justin could've heard a boutonniere pin drop in the stricken church. He glanced at his mother, sitting stoically in the front pew. No doubt she figured he had a plan to get the situation under control. But for the first time since his father died, leaving the job of diplomacy to him, Justin was at a loss for words.

He should probably start with an apology to his mother and permit her the *'I-told-you-so.'* She'd warned him time and time again about the damage Charlie could do to his reputation. He glanced at Morgan, picturing her missing tiara sitting atop her head. Apparently she didn't get the same lecture.

Sickness swirled in Justin's stomach, and a flash interrupted his speculative trance. The bright light drew his attention down the aisle to a large man with an even larger camera taking photos of the twirling flower girl. At least someone was having fun. But as soon as the sarcastic thought faded, another more ominous thought formed. That man, that camera, could ruin Justin by capturing an unsavory, unscripted moment and putting it on display.

Justin's chest clenched. He had a choice to make. He could either go through with what he once thought of as a politically advantageous wedding solely to save face and as a result, risk life with a duplicitous woman, or he could step back, take a breather and make certain he was doing the right thing by marrying a woman he didn't trust and didn't love simply to follow through on his father's promise.

With an inhale and an exhale, Justin raised his hands. "I need a minute."

"Don't you dare walk out on me," Morgan threatened through clenched teeth.

He hadn't thought about walking out until she suggested it, and now that she had, he wanted to. Walking wouldn't solve the big problem, but if he walked, nobody would see him blow. And for the first time in years, he heard the ticking of a time bomb with each beat of his heart.

Months' worth of frustration trapped between his cummerbund and bowtie. He'd allowed himself to be a pawn in a game his father started years ago. There were no more clandestine whiskey and cigar meetings between Marvin Mitchell and Robert Parrish, but their plans for power remained. If their dreams for political dominance had died along with Justin's father, Justin wouldn't be standing here today. But he was standing here, a willing accomplice, because as Marvin's oldest son, it was his duty to follow through with his father's best-laid plans, plans which included a Congressional seat and a loveless marriage.

Crazy? Maybe. But his father said powerful families arranged marriages all the time. They were business transactions of mutual benefit. In this case, Justin would get a beautiful, poised, politically-appropriate wife, who happened to come with a dowry of several hundred million dollars in the shape of an international plastics plant, and Morgan would get a wealthy husband with power, influence and title. Everybody won, unless, of course, you counted love, which Justin didn't. Love didn't win elections. Love didn't balance the measly budgets of rural Pennsylvania towns. Love was one of the few luxuries powerful people couldn't afford.

Or so he'd been told over and over again by the most unlikely source, his bride-to-be. He'd been focused and methodical about marrying Morgan for the power and stability her family could offer this town, and yet he stood here, shaken by the unknown. Was it possible Morgan had risked his reputation and all they planned to accomplish together by carrying on with Charlie?

When Justin looked at Morgan, she looked away.

On the first wave of impulse Justin had permitted in years, he threw up his hands. "I apologize, but this isn't going to happen today."

"I'll kill her," Morgan roared. So much for poise under pressure.

Any other time, Justin would've placated her for the sake of keeping appearances, but now he simply wanted to get away. He walked up the aisle with gasps and gossip to his back. He could only imagine his mother's fear and confusion. It was almost enough to turn him around. Almost.

"When I get my hands on that little … " Morgan's threats against Alice faded and somewhere in the distance a door slammed.

Justin didn't stop to see what happened. At the moment, he was too numb to care. His mind warned that this could be political suicide, but he needed the truth. Once he knew what Alice knew, he could form a plan.

He reached down to scoop up the pair of shoes that littered the aisle. Alice Cramer had given him grief since the day they first met. She had better have a damn good explanation now.

Other books by Elley Arden include:

Save My Soul

Change My Mind

Baby By Design

In the mood for more Crimson Romance?
Check out *Slow Ride* by Kat Morrisey at *CrimsonRomance.com*.